GLASS HOUSES

by

CARMEN K. GLENN

Edited by Suzanne Bailer Smith

First published by Dog Ear Publishing
4010 W. 86th Street, Ste H
Indianapolis, IN 46268
www.dogearpublishing.net

dog ear
PUBLISHING

ISBN: 978-145750-355-9

This book is printed on acid-free paper.

Printed in the United States of America

Also by Carmen K. Glenn

Overdrive

Ambition

Office Gossip

To my sisters, Kimberly Walker and Tamara Carmichael

Chapter 1

Throwing Stones

"Go ahead and shoot me if you think you have the balls!" Bianca shouts at Rachel, who is standing on the adjacent side of the cramped living room, while Kelli struggles frantically to wrestle the gun away. The oversized furniture in the tiny space leaves no room for the thrashing bodies to maneuver without bumping into the sofa or loveseat or tumbling over an accent piece.

"No, Rachel, you don't want it to end this way!" Kelli begs. "Think about your future, girl. You've got too much to live for! Think about your parents. This'll kill them! Your father's the pastor of a church. His only child can't spend the rest of her life in prison! Just think about it, please!" Kelli says, sweating profusely as she struggles in a tug-of-war with Rachel, who is at least four inches taller and more than fifty pounds heavier than she. The two have already knocked two pictures off the wall and tumbled over a plant resting on a delicate iron plant stand.

"Rachel, you don't want to disappoint Mrs. Pettigrew and Rev. Pettigrew, do you?" Bianca teases, using a four-year-old's whining voice instead of that of a grown woman. "Oh, no, not their perfect little daughter with all of her fancy education, successful career and big bank account. Why, that would just devastate the perfect Pettigrew family."

"Shut up! You're just jealous because you're ignorant, unemployed and broke!" Rachel yells back at Bianca, cutting her to the core.

"Whoa! Such nasty words coming from the good pastor's daughter. Where did you learn that type of language—in Sunday school or bible study?" Bianca asks with an evil smile spread wide across her face.

Rachel twists her face harshly and replies, "The same place you learned to be a prostitute—from your stepfather!"

Bianca takes the argument over the top by saying with a sad expression, "I'm surprised that a barren bitch like you could come up with something so clever, yet so low down."

"No more!" Kelli shouts. Facing Bianca, she demands, "Bianca, shut your mouth; just shut up!" Then, turning her attention to Rachel, she pleads, "Please, Rachel," as sweetly as honey dripping from her lips, yet never releasing her grip from the weapon. "Please put down the gun."

Instead of the surrender she hoped to get from Rachel, a long stream of tears begin to flow from Rachel's eyes, cascading her smeared mascara down her cheeks and splattering and discoloring her white silk blouse.

"She thinks I don't have the guts," Rachel says calmly. "She thinks I won't do it," she says in a near whisper. "But I will. I swear I'll kill her," Rachel says, resuming her effort to regain control of the gun. With one swift move, Rachel and Kelli knock over a crystal lamp from a side table. It crashes onto the hardwood floor breaking into a million tiny pieces.

As Rachel and Kelli fight for possession of the 9-millimeter handgun, Bianca stands in place, hands on hips, poking out her swollen belly that holds her first child due in less than one month. You would think in such a delicate condition, Bianca would set her butt down, shut her mouth and show some sense. But not her! Bianca has to show her behind, eight months pregnant and all.

All the while, Kelli wonders over and over again in her mind, *How did we get to this point? We all used to be best friends. We grew up on the same street and played together as children. Now here we are grown women and Rachel is waving a loaded gun around like it's a child's play toy. Bianca has the gall to egg Rachel on as if the gun is going to shoot out a stream of water instead of bullets that will cut through her flesh, destroying both Bianca and her unborn child. How have I let the two of them get me into the middle of their mess?"*

"Get out of the way, Kelli! You can't protect her now! This time she's gone too far! This time I'm going to kill this tramp and put her out of her misery!" Rachel demands.

Feeling like she's losing the battle for possession of the gun, Kelli turns to Bianca and yells, "Get out of here! I can't hold her back much longer. Get out of here now!"

A stubborn Bianca never removes her hands from her hips, never backs down. "I'm not going anywhere!" she announces defiantly. "Let her handle her business, Kelli. Let her do what she thinks she has to do!"

It's finally going down. Bianca and Rachel, who have been both friends and enemies since sixth grade, are finally going to end it all one way or another. Even if someone doesn't end up dying here today, how does a friendship recover after one friend has tried to kill the other?

Only fate could allow their relationship to end in the same place where it all began. It was in this exact spot where the three girls had met, the house where Kelli had grown up. It was the summer before the girls entered the sixth grade. Kelli and Rachel had lived next door to each other for several years prior and had been playmates since they were toddlers. The house on the other side of Kelli's had come up for rent. Most of the homeowners weren't happy about rental property springing up in the predominantly middle-class suburban area. Still, when the white couple moved into the rental property, Kelli's mother, Rita, baked a cake and welcomed the new family into the neighborhood anyway. Rita's mother had taught her good manners and Rita dusted them off and used them from time to time. When Rita discovered the new neighbors had a twelve-year-old daughter, she promptly brought the girl to her house and introduced Bianca to Kelli and Rachel, right in the middle of her living room.

Kelli and Rachel took one look at Bianca's mulatto skin, hazel brown eyes and kinky, sandy-brown hair, and knew right away that someone next door had slept with someone black to make this child. Rachel took one look at Bianca's long hair that was even longer than her own, the curves in Bianca's waist and hips, where she herself did not have any, and Bianca's perfect teeth, where hers were crooked and required braces, soon to be put in place, and she decided she hated Bianca. However, Rachel's father preached about loving thy neighbor, so she pretended to at least like Bianca, but deep down inside Rachel despised her.

Bianca and Kelli became instant friends. But, in order to play with Kelli, Bianca had to pretend to make nice with Rachel. Still, Bianca was convinced that Rachel looked like the "darkie" her mother claimed her black father had run off with. Bianca was convinced Rachel was the same "darkie" reincarnated. So it began, Bianca's and Rachel's lifetime of being both friends and enemies.

Now, nearly three decades later, all three women are forty years of age; things have not gotten much better between Bianca and Rachel. Today, someone will end up dead, in the same living room, where it all began so long ago.

Chapter 2
Kelli

28 *Years Ago*...Kelli Brown was the kind of pre-teen girl to whom neither adults nor children paid much attention. She was average height and weight, with a coffee brown complexion and average looks. Her mother, Rita, kept Kelli dressed in decent K-Mart clothes and well groomed. Still, there was nothing striking about her. Her dark coarse hair was maintained in its natural, kinky state, except for the rare occasions when Rita straightened it with a pressing comb. Two years prior, Kelli began wearing eye glasses, and the plain, dark frames only added to her mediocre appearance.

While she didn't require a training bra, Kelli wore one anyway, since most of the girls her age wore them and she was desperate to fit in. Kelli waited impatiently for her menstrual cycle because she wanted something to help her gain status with her peers. For the most part, Kelli was the kind of girl who blended in with the woodwork. If someone didn't point Kelli out, one might just as well walk right past without noticing her.

Kelli lived with her mother, Rita, and her father, Jackson, a traveling salesman who was on the road most of the time. By the time Kelli was entering the sixth grade, she still didn't understand what it was her father did while he traveled. He never brought his work home, on the rare occasion when he did come home and he kept very few belongings in the house. He didn't even have tools in the garage like all of her friends' fathers; not even so much as a lawn mower. There was a teenager down the street who cut their grass in the spring and summer and Rita paid him. The same boy returned in the fall to rake leaves and again, in the winter, to shovel snow.

Kelli's curiosity about her father's occupation grew tremendously. This grew especially so after going into the office with Rita one Saturday morning, while her mother caught up on some of her secretarial duties. Kelli had been intrigued by the typewriter Rita used to crank out documents so quickly, and the photo copier that spit out perfectly copied forms on warm paper. Kelli loved the stapler, paper cutter and the dozens of ink pens stashed in Rita's desk.

Even at such a young age, Kelli knew exactly how her mother had gotten behind in her work duties. After Rita had been drinking alone at home until she got drunk, she would get behind in household chores as well; like washing dishes, mopping floors and cooking meals. Kelli didn't mind, because by then she was old enough to pick up the slack. She could fix a peanut-butter-and-jelly sandwich until Rita sobered up.

However, like clock work, Rita was always sober enough each Sunday afternoon to visit her mother in the rest home. Grammy had been in that same Senior Citizen's Center for many years. Each Sunday, the two would dress in their very best, cheap clothes. Rita was always certain to place the simple gold band on the ring finger of her left hand for the visit, as she did for most social occasions. Each week, Rita and Kelli would see for themselves how Grammy's mind and body had deteriorated since the week before.

"How was church service?" Grammy would ask them in her weakened voice that seemed to match the condition of her body. Grammy could barely hold her head up on her own. She was always in the hospital bed in her room of the rest home. She never sat in the visiting area like many of the other elderly residents.

"Reverend Pettigrew preached a marvelous service this Sunday," Rita would reply each time. Sometimes Rita would even tell Grammy the topic of the sermon or the passage from which the pastor preached. Rita could do this easily because she had been reared in the church and knew the bible well.

Kelli occasionally stumbled when sharing her pretend Sunday school lesson with Grammy. This made Rita nervous and she would sometimes give Kelli a light kick, when Grammy's head was turned or her eyes were shut. Kelli learned to quickly get her story back on track.

In reality, Rita and Kelli only went to church services on Easter, Mother's Day and Christmas. Rita said it was okay to tell little white lies to Grammy to make her feel better. There were a number of little white lies they told Grammy, like Rita's tale about being a housewife. Kelli thought Rita was ashamed of being a secretary, but Kelli found her mother's job fascinating.

Rita would go on and on to Grammy about preparing fabulous meals for her family, when a trip to McDonalds or Burger Chef was their customary dinner. Sometimes they both told Grammy tales about family vacations they never went on. Going to visit Grammy was a game they played. Rita never explained the game to Kelli, but Kelli somehow learned to play it well.

There were even more tales about Jackson, Rita's husband. According to Rita, Jackson could fix anything around the house. The month prior, she said Jackson had fixed the washing machine, although Kelli distinctly remembered washing clothes by hand until Mr. Williams, who lives two doors down from their house, replaced a part on the washer and the machine started spinning again.

Rita updated Grammy on every aspect of the upkeep of the house. Rightfully so, as the house Rita and Kelli lived in was owned by Grammy and her late husband, who died before Kelli was born. Listening to Rita's stories, one would think the house was in pristine condition instead of hanging on by a needle and thread.

Still, one white lie turned into another and then another. Rita and Kelli worked hard to keep the white lies straight. Kelli really wanted to help make Grammy feel better, but why they had to tell so many untruths was all a mystery to her. Particularly, the lies about Kelli's father, Jackson, were the most mysterious of all the white lies they told to Grammy.

Chapter 3
Rachel

Rachel Pettigrew was one of the most popular girls at her school and in the community. She and Kelli had lived next door to each other since they were young children and the two played together almost daily. Rachel's father, Rev. Pettigrew, was one of few black ministers in Fairfield, Ohio. With the city's beloved minister for a father and a stay-at-home mother, Rachel, their only child, was raised like royalty.

Rachel was the type of child who could not and would not be ignored. She was always tall for her age, with brilliant dark skin, exotic, dark-brown eyes and long, thick black hair, to which Mrs. Ophelia Pettigrew applied a chemical relaxer by the time she was five years old. Rachel was always dressed in the very best department store clothes and that, too, made her appear a few years beyond her maturity level. By the summer before the sixth grade began, Rachel left her training bra behind for a real bra, and her butt had already grown larger than Mrs. Pettigrew's.

Most of the boys in junior high, and a few in high school, started to notice Rachel and her budding figure. Rev. and Mrs. Pettigrew noticed the attention their daughter was attracting and rarely let the child out of their sight. Yet, it didn't stop Rachel from having her first kiss in the fifth grade in the basement of the church during morning service. While her father preached on the topic of "Children, Obey Your Parents in The Lord," Rachel excused herself to go to the restroom. Instead of doing her business in the ladies' room, Rachel met Darren Jenkins, a boy in the eighth grade, in the Sunday school classroom. Mrs. Pettigrew noticed when Rachel returned to the sanctuary that she was missing the cherry-flavored, lip smacker gloss. Rachel always kept the lip moisturizer spread thick across her lips, resembling Crisco oil. From that point on, Mrs. Pettigrew started watching Rachel like a hawk.

Rev. and Mrs. Pettigrew held a high position in the community and it was Mrs. Pettigrew's job to ensure their image was not tarnished by anyone, not even Rachel. So, although Rachel had been promoted to the sixth grade, she was not permitted to walk to the corner convenience store with Kelli or any of her other friends. Rachel protested there were kids as young as the third grade allowed to walk to the store unaccompanied by an adult. Mrs. Pettigrew responded, "I will not have a child of mine appearing so low class. You are the daughter of Rev. Pettigrew and you will not be seen walking to the convenience store like one of these fatherless children in this community!" Rachel knew Mrs. Pettigrew's comment was a direct jab at Kelli, her best friend, whose father was practically never at home. Still, Rachel yearned to have the same basic freedom her peers enjoyed. In her eyes it was embarrassing to watch the other children walk to the convenience store for an ice cream cone or a pack of Now and Laters and she was not permitted to join them, although she nearly appeared to be a young adult.

Rev. and Mrs. Pettigrew owned two cars, and if Rachel required something from the store, then she was driven there like a proper young lady by Mrs. Pettigrew. This did not completely satisfy Rachel. Yet, from that point on, anything Rachel was not permitted to do, she simply stated the activity was "low class." This included walking to the park, the skating rink and the movie theatre with the other kids in the neighborhood. Since this was the entirety of her friends' activities, everyone thought Rachel was stuck up, but no one dared say so, because the community revered Rev. Pettigrew.

Chapter 4
Bianca

Bianca Goode was born to a Caucasian mother and black father. So this made Bianca bi-racial, mulatto, mixed, African-American or whatever term she thought was most in fashion. As much as she tried to make her light skin and kinky hair fit into the equation, there was no fitting in for a girl like Bianca in the small Ohio town where the family landed. The town was too conservative, backwards or just plain old ignorant to fully accept a child like Bianca, who was now being raised by her mother and white step-father. Bianca was the only one who looked like her in her family. Her four younger siblings were blonde-haired and blue-eyed like their father. This made Bianca stick out like a sore thumb.

Bianca's mother, April Goode, was more of a hindrance than a help in the situation. When April started dating Mr. Goode she told him Bianca's father had been a very dark Italian man, to explain the child's dark skin and kinky hair. Mr. Goode was so smitten by April he never questioned the story. It wasn't until after they were married and Mr. Goode had given the fatherless child his last name that he learned the truth. Still, April was prepared to hold on to the marriage. She made sure she was already pregnant by then. Mr. Goode would certainly not abandon a pure white child of his own.

Mr. Goode didn't leave his wife and unborn child, but he did treat Bianca like the nappy-headed step-child she was. Mr. Goode and April both showed little love to Bianca. The child didn't hold the status of the oldest child in the family; that was left for the oldest son of Mr. Goode and April. Instead, Bianca was given the leftovers and scraps. If there was money left over after buying the other children new shoes, then Bianca would get new shoes. If there was no money left over, then Bianca continued to wear her old shoes. Not that a lot of shoe buying went on in the Goode household. For the most part, the family struggled. They always lived on the edge. If one child had to be sacrificed, you could be sure Bianca would be the first to go.

The only love Bianca received at home came from the youngest Goode child, Lilly. Now almost two years old, she had adored Bianca almost since the day she was born. Bianca's embrace was often the only thing that would soothe the crying baby. When Lilly was sick, Bianca was the only one who could get the baby to take a spoonful of medicine. Lilly loved her big sister. Mr. Goode and April noticed how attached Lilly was to Bianca, and he took to referring to Bianca as Lilly's mammy. That was only one of the many ways Mr. Goode expressed his resentment toward Bianca.

The worst of the ill treatment came just before the Goode family moved next door to Kelli and Rita. Mr. Goode started sneaking into Bianca's bedroom at night. Bianca was confused. The man who never hugged her, never had a kind word for her and was quick to tell her she wasn't his child, loved to lie atop her on the twin-sized bed. He came all the way downstairs to her tiny room off the kitchen where she slept. How he moaned and groaned with such pleasure and smiled when he was done. Why had he wanted to keep such a secret with Bianca, although he seemed not to like her?

The move into the new house would certainly stop the secret she shared with Mr. Goode, or so Bianca thought. Her mother had told her she would be sharing a bedroom with her two half-sisters in the new house. Bianca was certain Mr. Goode would not be climbing on top of her in the middle of the night anymore. He wouldn't want his precious daughters to know about their secret. Besides, Bianca would be starting her menstrual cycle soon, and April had told her she would be able to make babies after that. Her mother was very clear that Bianca had better not make a baby while she was still living in Mr. Goode's house.

In reality, April did not want Bianca to make the same mistake she had. April gave birth to Bianca when she was just sixteen years old and promptly dropped out of high school. April's parents immediately kicked her out of the house when she gave birth to the kinky-haired infant. Even then, April tried her best to deny the true paternity of her child. April was eighteen and living on welfare in a rented room in Hamilton, Ohio, when she met Mr. Goode.

April always said, "Thank God for Mr. Goode. He rescued us from hell."

There were no more government checks and food stamps after April married Mr. Goode, but other things weren't quite plentiful either. The family moved every few years from trailer park to trailer park until Mr. Goode scraped enough money together to rent a house for the family. All of the children were excited about having a yard all their own in which to play. Bianca was excited about the prospect of no longer sharing the secret with Mr. Goode.

Chapter 5

Laying The Foundation

The day Kelli, Rachel and Bianca were introduced, the three girls found themselves playing a game of jacks on Rita's living room floor. Kelli had made it to the set of fives on her first turn and now Rachel was fast approaching on her set of threes.

"So how many brothers and sisters you got, Bianca?" Kelli asked as she waited for Rachel to complete her turn.

"Two half-brothers and two half-sisters," Bianca replied.

Kelli had never heard of a half-brother/sister, so she asked, "Why do you call them half brothers and sisters?"

Bianca opened her mouth to respond, but Rachel jumped in rudely.

"You're so stupid, Kelli! It means they don't have the same mother and father. They share only one parent with Bianca. That was a low-class question to ask."

Kelli rolled her eyes at Rachel. Rachel had been in the habit of calling everything *low-class* and frankly, Kelli was getting sick of it.

"Yeah, we all have the same mother, but Mr. Goode is their father, not mine," Bianca replied, hanging her head low, tired of twelve years of the shame of not having a father to speak of.

"Why do you call their father Mr. Goode? Won't he let you call him *Daddy*?" Kelli asked.

Bianca pretended to observe Rachel intently as she spread the jacks out on the floor to complete her set of threes. "I don't know," Bianca replied, as she shrugged her shoulders. "I've always called him Mr. Goode."

Before Rachel attempted to pick up the three sets of threes and the remaining single jack, she added, "Not everyone calls their parents by their first names, like you do, Rita and Jackson." Then she added, "That's so disrespectful."

Kelli shot back, "And not everybody calls their parents Mrs. So and So and Rev. So and So," as she rolled her eyes toward the ceiling.

Kelli's comment, coupled with her eye-rolling, made Bianca giggle. Rachel ended her threes and began her fours. Kelli knew Rachel would never make it through her fours on the first attempt. She never had before in the history of jacks. Sure enough, with Kelli and Bianca looking on, Rachel tripped up and missed two of the four jacks she attempted to pick up.

"I hate to say it Bianca, but you're a jinx! I never mess up on my fours!" Rachel announced.

Kelli pursed her lips and cocked her head to the side. "Rachel Ann Pettigrew, you are telling a story before God and everybody! You always mess up on your fours. If I hear another lie come out of your mouth, I'm telling Rev. Pettigrew!"

"Shut up, Kelli! You get on my nerves. You're always telling on somebody!" Rachel said hastily.

"Not somebody you!" Kelli corrected her. In the same motion, Kelli swept up the ten jacks and the ball from the floor and handed them to Bianca. "Your turn," she said to her new friend.

Bianca's eyes lit up. She took the jacks from Kelli's hand and right away she completed her ones, twos and threes before she took in a breath. Rachel looked on intently, because she didn't want this new girl getting ahead of her so quickly. Yet, Bianca continued without making a mistake. She completed her fours, fives and sixes perfectly. Kelli and Rachel looked on, astonished as Bianca passed them both by. Without hesitation, Bianca breezed through her sevens, eights, nines and tens.

After she won the game, Bianca took a deep breath and looked up at Rachel. Rachel hated to lose and she frowned at Bianca, rolling her eyes at the girl. Bianca was accustomed to harsh looks, so Rachel's grimacing didn't bother her. Yet, when Bianca turned her attention to Kelli, Kelli was grinning from ear to ear. Kelli was glad Bianca had beat Rachel hands down, putting Rachel in her place. Bianca joined Kelli with a smile of her own.

Rachel ended the game. "I hate jacks. It's a low-class game anyway!"

That was the first and last time the three girls played jacks together.

Chapter 6
Kelli

A few weeks into summer vacation Jackson arrived home and announced a week-long stay. Kelli was excited that her father would be at home for so long. She was confident this would give her enough time to talk him into taking her on the road with him. So, right away, Kelli began to share with her father all of her experiences at Rita's job.

"And Rita has a work badge she shows the security officer to get inside the building. It has her picture on it and everything. Do you have a badge like that, Jackson?"

Jackson smiled at his daughter from across the dinner table, his cocoa-brown skin and dimples in his cheeks matching hers. "Yes, I have a work badge, too, Sweetheart."

"Can I see it?" Kelli wanted to know desperately.

Jackson hesitated. "I'll be sure to get it out and show it to you before the end of the week."

"Maybe you could take me on the road with you this time when you leave," Kelli hinted.

"What has Jackson told you, Kelli?" Rita asked her daughter.

Kelli didn't respond, although she knew exactly what Rita was referring to. Instead, Kelli pretended to dig into the spaghetti and meatballs sitting in a large heap on her plate.

"Kelli, you know Jackson is very busy when he's on the road. He doesn't have time to baby-sit you," Rita scolded.

"But I'm almost twelve-years-old. I don't need a babysitter anymore. Besides, you let me stay at home by myself when you go to work now," Kelli reminded Rita.

"Only because Mrs. Pettigrew is right next door to keep an eye on you," Rita stated.

"Don't worry, Sweetheart," Jackson said softly, "I'll be sure that we do something special this week while I'm home."

Jackson didn't make many promises, but when he did, Kelli knew his word was as good as gold. Kelli's mind began to race. There were dozens of things that she would love to do with Jackson. They rarely had the opportunity to spend any real father-daughter time alone. Kelli loved her father and wanted desperately to be a daddy's girl, only if Jackson were around more.

"How about an amusement park!" Kelli blurted out. She had gone to an amusement park in Cincinnati with the church. She thought it would be great to go with her very own father.

"Well, the closest park is in Cincinnati, and that's a long drive," Jackson explained.

"It's not so long. We went with the church last summer. A whole bus load of kids and a few chaperones."

"How about we try doing something a bit more calm," Jackson said, as he looked to Rita for assistance.

Kelli noticed the look Rita returned to Jackson. It was the same look Rita exchanged with Kelli on their visits with Grammy, when they were playing their game. Kelli silently wondered if Rita and Jackson were playing a game on her.

"How about a drive-in movie," Rita suggested.

Although Kelli thought it was a lame plan, she went along reluctantly. A trip to the drive-in movie was better than nothing at all. Even though the plan had turned out to be a family outing, at least it gave Kelli something to look forward to. Besides, she could brag to Rachel about seeing a few of the latest movies, knowing Rachel's family never went to the drive-in at all.

After dinner Kelli headed to the living room to watch an episode of *Diff'rent Strokes*. It was her favorite television program and she never missed it. She turned the television set on and plopped down on the sofa, while Rita washed dishes in the kitchen and Jackson went to the back porch to smoke a Marlboro. As Kelli sat on the sofa, adjacent to her on the coffee table were Jackson's car keys and wallet. She was anxious to see his work I.D., so without a second thought, she picked up the wallet and opened it.

Kelli spotted a card with Jackson's picture on it. After careful inspection, Kelli realized the card was not a work I.D., but a driver's license. Kelli pulled the driver's license from Jackson's wallet. She froze as she saw that Jackson's last name was not Brown, like hers and Rita's. Instead, his name was Jackson Carter. If that were not mysterious enough, Jackson's home address was not the address where Rita and Kelli lived. Instead it was 1524 Grant Circle in Fairfield, Ohio. The image of the driver's license bore a hole into Kelli's soul.

Kelli returned the wallet to the coffee table next to the sofa. She sat like a zombie through her favorite TV show. To this day, she could not recall which episode aired that evening or how many times Gary Coleman delivered his infamous line, "What you talkin' 'bout, Willis?" Kelli continued to wonder for years to come who Jackson Carter really was and why he lived at another address in the same town where she and Rita lived.

Chapter 7
Rachel

Rachel sat fuming on the passenger side of her mother's white Chevrolet Caprice Classic. Her lips were poked out and every time Ophelia Pettigrew made a comment, Rachel rolled her eyes at her mother. Half way to the orthodontist's office Rachel turned her body toward the passenger door window, refusing to look at Ophelia at all.

"Rachel Ann, that is no way to act towards your very own mother! Rev. Pettigrew would be appalled!" Ophelia admonished her only child.

"I'm appalled I have to get braces on my teeth. This is going to ruin the next two years of my life!" Rachel tells her mother, never bothering to turn her body around from the passenger door window.

"Rachel, Dear, you need to count your blessings." Ophelia started in with a softer approach.

"Your teeth are crooked and Rev. Pettigrew can afford to put braces on them to straighten them out. You should be grateful for that. It'll be a small inconvenience for the next two years, but you'll have a beautiful smile for a lifetime."

"My teeth aren't that bad. Rev. Pettigrew just wants to make my life miserable."

"Now, Rachel, you know that's not true. Getting braces is no big deal. You're just acting like a big baby."

Rachel and Ophelia rode in silence for the remainder of the trip. By the time they arrived in the parking lot of the orthodontist's office, Rachel decided she would not be getting a mouth full of embarrassing metal placed on her teeth. Ophelia turned off the car's engine, placing the keys in her pocketbook, and turned to Rachel.

"Come on now, young lady," Ophelia instructed Rachel.

"No, Mrs. Pettigrew, I won't do it!" Rachel said and grabbed the passenger-door handle. "I won't let you do this to me!"

By that time Ophelia had had enough of Rachel's behavior. The ungrateful preteen had finally backed her into a corner. Still, she couldn't return home without the braces applied to Rachel's teeth. Rev. Pettigrew would be furious indeed. Not to mention, Ophelia had already told many of the sisters from church that Rachel would be getting braces. She knew many of them were envious because they wished to get braces for their own children, but could not afford them.

In the sweetest and most nurturing voice, Ophelia pleaded, "Dear, turn around and let me talk to you."

Still, Rachel maintained the vice-like hold on the automobile door. She would not give up easily, if at all.

"Come on, Sweetheart." Ophelia pleaded. "You be nice to Mother and Mother will be nice to you."

Rachel knew her mother was on the verge of offering her a delicious bribe to let go of the car door and enter the doctor's office. Rachel was determined to hold out for the best possible deal.

"Come on, Dear," Ophelia crooned once more in peace.

Finally, Rachel released her tight grip on the passenger-door handle and turned to face her mother.

"I know this is difficult for you, Rachel, but it will pay off in the end. I promise you it will."

Dead silence fell between the two. Neither of them did more than breathe and both of them maintained their position firmly; the only difference being, Ophelia Pettigrew was raised in the ghetto and she had a few more tricks up her sleeve than Rachel, her suburban daughter, could ever imagine.

"Come here, Dear." Ophelia extended her arms toward Rachel. As Rachel closed her eyes and leaned into her mother's warm embrace, she was shocked when she felt the contrast of a harsh, stinging slap across her face. Rachel's eyes opened widely, and before her appeared a self-assured Ophelia Pettigrew.

"Now, don't you ever think about defying me again," Ophelia said, while twisting her neck and speaking in a tone Rachel had never heard her use before.

Rachel exited the car and went inside the orthodontist's office. She sat quietly as the metal braces were applied to her teeth. Rachel never spoke to a living soul about the slap she received that day, but she never forgot it either.

Chapter 8

Bianca

The first few weeks in the new house were fairly good for Bianca. She and her mother spent all of their time arranging the family's meager belongings inside the house. Bianca had even been permitted a few times to play with Kelli, her new best friend next door. The excitement of having a real friend was almost more than Bianca could contain.

One evening after dinner, April took the family's broken-down station wagon to the corner grocery store to pick up a gallon of milk for the next morning's breakfast. With five children in the house, milk was a precious commodity which had to be purchased often. April took the two younger girls with her and left Bianca at home to wash the dinner dishes. As Bianca did her chores, she was interrupted by Mr. Goode.

"Bianca, bring the broom upstairs and sweep the floor," Mr. Goode said, looking around suspiciously. His sons were in the living room in front of the only television in the house, but clearly within hearing distance.

"Okay," Bianca answered nervously, never looking the six-feet, four-inches tall Mr. Goode in the eyes. "I'll be done with the dishes in just a minute."

"No. I want the floor swept right now," he said sternly. "Before your mother gets back," he added.

"Yes, Sir," Bianca responded. Yet, her mind turned over and over again. There had to be a way she could avoid being alone with Mr. Goode. This was their new house and she didn't want their awful secret to continue here. She wanted things to be different.

Still, with Mr. Goode staring at her and waiting impatiently for her to climb the steps, Bianca reached inside the broom closet, removing the broom. Mr. Goode led the way up the stairs. Half-way up the staircase, Bianca turned around. "I forgot the dustpan," she said, and headed back to the kitchen. When she entered the kitchen, instead of reaching inside the broom closet, Bianca stepped inside, squeezing her small frame in alongside the mop, bucket and other cleaning supplies. It was a tight fit, but Bianca managed to close the door. She heard the booming sound of Mr. Goode, as he called her name once, and then twice. She closed her eyes tight in the darkness of the closet and waited. She didn't hear him call her name a third time. Instead, the closet door opened and Mr. Goode was standing in front of her with his bright, blue eyes piercing through her body.

Bianca stepped out of the broom closet and nervously explained, "The door closed on me when I came down to get the dustpan." The excuse even sounded silly to her, but she was reaching for anything at all to get herself out of the predicament.

"Get the dustpan and come on up," Mr. Goode said sharply.

Bianca grabbed the dustpan and followed Mr. Goode to the top of the steps. She began busying herself with sweeping intently in the hallway between all three bedrooms. Mr. Goode sat on the edge of his large bed and stared at Bianca.

"Sweep the floor in here," he demanded of her.

Bianca was trapped. She had no way of escaping the inevitable. She slowly walked inside Mr. Goode's bedroom and began to sweep the floor unhurriedly, keeping her eyes focused downward on the imaginary pile of dirt she accumulated. Before she knew it, Mr. Goode closed and locked the bedroom door, and his hands were upon her. Bianca inhaled a deep breath as he touched her in places where a man should never touch a child. She did not exhale until Mr. Goode was done with her.

Chapter 9
Plumbing

Rachel was the first of the group of friends to start her menstrual cycle. She wore the distinct privilege like a badge of honor she had earned from years of meticulous planning, instead of the natural change in a young girl's body that it was.

"So, how does it feel?" Kelli asked, as she and Bianca sat on the side of Rachel's white canopy bed, staring at Rachel, who lay flat on her back, like she had contracted the Black Plague instead of having gotten her period.

"I don't know." Rachel responded, shifting around to get comfortable in the full size bed. She propped up her pillow and pretended to struggle to lift her aching body to a sitting position. "It's hard to describe how it feels to go from one day being a child to the next day becoming a full-grown woman." Rachel loved the attention and wanted Kelli and Bianca to envy her for her accomplishment.

A wide-eyed Bianca sheepishly asked, "Does it hurt?"

Rachel placed one hand over her abdomen and dramatically explained, "The pain is horrible. I didn't know what was happening to me. I thought I had some type of fire burning inside of me. Mrs. Pettigrew said I have cramps. She gave me an aspirin and said I'll be bed-ridden during this whole week every month."

"Bed ridden because of your period?" Kelli had some knowledge of menstruation from Rita. "That's stupid. Having a period doesn't make you bed-ridden!"

"I'm speaking from experience," Rachel assured Kelli.

"But it's summer vacation. You have to miss it stuck in bed because you're bleeding between your legs? That's stupid! Rita never said anything about staying in bed when I get my period."

Frustrated, Rachel raised her voice at Kelli, "When a woman gets *the curse*, it changes her whole life! There's no more time for child's play! It's time to grow up! A woman has to take care of her hygiene!"

"Hygiene?" Bianca repeated, looking from Rachel to Kelli hoping for an explanation.

"Yes, hygiene. Bianca, you're so low class!" Rachel shouted. "It means I have to change my sanitary pad. I can't sit around playing jacks like you kids. I have to tend to my hygiene."

"Well, there's no way I'm staying in bed everyday, when I get my period," Kelli said, folding her arms defiantly and looking away from Rachel.

"Look, Kelli. I'm telling you the truth about *the curse*. This is a woman's burden. It even says so in the Bible. I can't help it if Rita didn't tell you the truth; but this is what the two of you have to look forward to."

"Are you calling Rita a liar?" Kelli shouted defensively.

"I'm just saying, Rita didn't tell you the whole truth, because she knows what a baby you can be at times."

"A baby?" Kelli responded. "Who's lying in the bed like a baby now?"

"And who's trying to show off in front of Bianca?" Rachel retorted.

The girls looked up in time to see Rev. Pettigrew appear in the doorway of Rachel's bedroom. The preacher, being both tall and wide, filled the entire space of the doorway. His small, wire-rimmed glasses could easily be seen in contrast against his dark, chocolate skin as they rested on his broad nose.

"Is everything okay, girls?" his low, deep voice inquired.

"Hello, Rev. Pettigrew," Kelli and Bianca said in unison.

"Everything's fine, Rev. Pettigrew," Rachel responded in a weakened voice. "Kelli and Bianca just came over to check on me."

"Well, keep it down in here if you don't mind, young ladies," the good Reverend requested peacefully.

"Yes, Reverend Pettigrew," the three girls said in unison as the man of the house turned and walked away.

Kelli turned toward Rachel just long enough to roll her eyes and confirm once more in a hushed voice, "You're so stupid!"

Rachel gave up the argument and slowly lay back on the bed. She directed the remainder of her information on *the curse* to Bianca, who soaked up the information like a sponge. By the time Rachel was done, the impressionable Bianca was scared out of her mind at the thought of starting her menstrual cycle.

Chapter 10
Kelli

Sixth grade came and went and still Kelli had not come on her period. She carried a purse with her all school year with little more inside than the single sanitary napkin she was dying to use. The effort Kelli made to strap the purse across her shoulder each day, the energy she used to tote it all day long at school, especially when she switched classes to art, gym and music class, was in vain.

Womanhood evaded her. There were no growing bumps on her chest to fill her training bra and no menstrual cycle to announce to her small group of friends. Kelli's only highlight was being a sixth-grade, school crossing guard. It was an honor given to only the best of the best students. Only those students with a combination of high academic standards and good behavior were considered.

Wearing the florescent orange vest and holding the red "Stop" sign in front of the cars at the traffic light was her greatest childhood honor.

Kelli began to imagine she was one of Charlie's Angels, placed on special assignment at Cloverdale Elementary School to protect the children from reckless drivers. Kelli daydreamed of saving dozens of students from near death. In her mind, as crazy speeding drivers approached the cross walk, Kelli would scoop up an innocent child into her bosom. With a quick roll, landing safely on the curb of the street, while narrowly escaping danger, Kelli would become an instant heroine. All of the teachers and parents would be eternally grateful for her bravery and skill.

As the school year progressed, so did Kelli's daydreams. Kelli's imagination found herself foiling a plot by a group of students as they attempted to hold up the cafeteria lady at gun point. As the students, dressed in all black with stocking masks, rushed inside the cafeteria, Kelli would jump into action. Effortlessly karate-kicking each of the bad guys, she'd take away their guns, rendering them helpless. She imagined the entire cafeteria of students standing up and cheering for her. Also, the cafeteria ladies would be so grateful they would give her free lunches for the remainder of the school year.

This would especially make Rita happy. Each week, just prior to payday, Rita's funds were consistently low and she would end up counting out a hand full of pennies to pay for Kelli's lunch. The lunch lady would hold up the long line counting each coin to ensure Kelli had enough money to purchase the meal. Her brave heroics would eliminate having to endure that type of embarrassment.

Thankfully, each time Kelli placed on the crossing-guard vest, she escaped to her daydreams and became enthralled in the excitement. In her mind, she transformed into Wonder Woman, the Bionic Woman and Oh Mighty Isis at the drop of a hat. There was no caper too big or too small. She was always in the right place at the right time and she was always the heroine.

Unfortunately, all of that was only in her mind. Actually, the most excitement Kelli had as a crossing-guard was when some of the older students dared to cross against the traffic light or walked outside of the crosswalk lines. She nearly froze her buns off in the winter, and her hair frizzed into an Angela Davis Afro whenever it rained. In reality, the job wasn't glamorous, but it was something she could call her own.

Chapter 11
Rachel

Her year in sixth-grade was when Rachel secured a hall monitor position. After all, who wouldn't entrust the daughter of the town's beloved pastor with the honorable rank. Her plans quickly developed in the year of retribution. Rachel had plans even before the school year was underway to pay back all of the two-faced girls who had done even the slightest bit of dirt to her. There was a small group of girls who had taken it upon themselves to call her Bertha Butt. Those wenches would definitely make the list.

Moreover, there was one girl in particular at the top of her list—Tawana Tucker. Rachel was determined to send the grotesque girl marching to the principal's office with mud on her face the very first week of school. She owed Tawana a big payback from a recess incident that had occurred the previous spring.

Tawana was a giant; taller than all of the other children her age and most of her teachers. She had the strength of a full grown man and she used it to toss around the other kids like they were Raggedy Ann and Andy dolls. During an intense game of tetherball, Rachel had nearly defeated 'The Giant' and put Tawana Tucker in her place once and for all. Rachel was in the middle of winding the rope around the pole at an incredible speed. Her arms whipped through the air, hitting the ball on the end of the rope like a child possessed. The win would be a victory not just for Rachel, but for all fifth graders!

Rachel's long hair blew in the wind and her spring jacket was tucked snuggly around her waist. Rachel had transformed into a mighty hitting, tetherball machine. The other kids waiting in line cheered for Rachel. No one had ever come so close to beating Tawana Tucker in any game of physical challenge and now it looked as if Rachel Pettigrew was going to be their savior.

Out of nowhere, Tawana threw both of her meaty arms into the air in a double block. When the ball hit the giant arms, known as 'the wall of steel,' it bounced back and hit Rachel dead in the center of her forehead. Rachel stumbled from the harsh force of the impact, fell flat on her behind, and watched helplessly as Tawana Tucker unwound the rope she had worked so hard to get into position. With minimal effort, Tawana slapped the ball with one swift blow and the rope flew around the pole in 'The Giant's' favor until she reached victory.

Rachel's near-fame was overshadowed by the sizeable purple bruise on her forehead. She walked around with the anomaly for an entire week, that incident going down in history as the longest week of Rachel's young life.

Rachel would repay Tawana Tucker and all the kids who laughed at her during that fiasco. She would catch that overgrown giant in a hall violation if it was the last thing she did. Rachel would go so far as to tell a lie on Tawana if she had to, in order to exact her revenge.

Chapter 12
Bianca

It wasn't easy for Bianca in the new school and the new town. She was darker than all of the white children and lighter than the black children. She was stuck in the middle, and frankly, if it had not been for Kelli, she would have been completely on her own. On rare occasions Rachel befriended Bianca at school, but only at times when it suited Rachel's needs. Bianca struggled to find her place among her peers, teachers and neighbors.

If someone thought Bianca's mulatto skin was pretty, then Rachel was right there at Bianca's side. Rachel thought she was, of course, in good with all of the beautiful people. However, if Bianca was being ridiculed for wearing second hand clothes, Rachel walked past the girl, as if she never saw her before in her life. Always, Kelli remained a true-blue friend in good times and in bad. Kelli never joined in when a group of kids came together to tease Bianca about her light skin and nappy hair.

Whites in the small town had already decided how they felt about blacks, and blacks had decided how they felt about whites. Prejudice thrived in the tiny Midwest town. Some despised the others. Yet, what about a child like her? Was she white? Was she black? Or was she something even worse, because her white mother had lain with a black man? People put her in different categories, and their feelings for Bianca in the community ranged from love to hate.

It impacted the entire Goode family. It impacted how the other parents behaved toward April Goode when she attended a PTA meeting. It dictated how the Goode children were regarded in the neighborhood and at school. It made Mr. Goode hot under the collar when he received negative repercussions at work. It set him on fire when it happened at the tiny hole-in-the-wall bar where he drank beer on Friday nights. He would come home hotter than a firecracker!

"That girl started trouble for me again!" he would yell at April. "She done made a bad situation worse for me. I'm already struggling to make ends meet and now she gone and caused those guys at work to start looking at me sideways, like

I did somethin' wrong. It ain't my fault her skin is dark. I didn't have nothin' to do wit' it!"

He accused her as though Bianca actually had something to do with the color of her own skin, the texture of her hair, and the biological parents to whom she was born. If only Mr. Goode knew how badly Bianca wished she could change the circumstances in which she was brought into the world. She would give anything to have a place where she felt she belonged. She desperately wanted to be cherished. While the love she received from her baby sister, Lily, was the only ray of sunshine in her home, it alone was not enough. She desired appreciation from the rest of her family. If that was too much to ask, at the very least, she thought she deserved some common decency.

Chapter 13

Chimney Smoke

The summer before Junior High School began, the girls shared a half-pack of Marlboros in Kelli's garage. The garage was unattached to the house, set at the back of the property and was nearly covered by large trees. So, although, Kelli's home set between Rachel's and Bianca's, the garage was a good place for the girls to go and have some privacy.

Lucky for them, Jackson had abandoned the cigarettes on the back porch during his last occasion at home, which was not unusual. Jackson was infamous for having an open pack of cigarettes in his shirt pocket, his pants pocket, on the passenger side of his car, on the nightstand in the bedroom, on the kitchen countertop, on the living room cocktail table and basically, everywhere he would leave them. He alone smoked enough cigarettes to keep Philip Morris Co. in business.

Kelli sat on a green-and-white striped, plastic lawn chair, puffing away like a pro. "You know all the cool people in junior high smoke. That's why the two of you babies have to learn to do it right. I don't want you to embarrass yourselves," she said, as she flicked her ashes into an empty soda pop bottle.

Bianca looked up from the can of paint she was sitting on and tried not to choke on the smoke filling her lungs. "You don't have to worry about me. I smoked a cigarette before," she said self-assuredly.

"Oh yeah, when?" A frustrated Rachel asked with an incredulous expression on her face, as she balanced her weight on a stack of boxes marked "yard sale." Rachel had not been successful at operating the lighter.

"At our old house," Bianca replied. "Mr. Goode's mother showed me how to light her cigarette on the stove. Once, when she asked me to light one and bring it to her in the front room, I took a couple of puffs of it. It was no big deal, really."

Kelli removed the cigarette from her mouth and blew out a long stream of smoke. "I bet she would die if she knew your black lips touched her cigarettes."

"Granny Goode don't mind me being mixed."

"And if she did, so what," Rachel said, barely audible, holding her unlit cigarette between her lips and still trying to operate the Bic lighter.

"I don't care who can't accept me being mixed. I am what I am," Bianca said nonchalantly.

Rachel glanced in Bianca's direction and stated, "So now you're talking like Popeye."

"Grow up!" Bianca retorted. "Why don't you concentrate on lighting that cigarette, *Bertha Butt*?"

Rachel did not take kindly to Bianca calling her the insulting name kids at school used to tease her, and Rachel twisted her neck and rolled her eyes when she replied nastily, "Don't make me come over there and smack the black off you, half-breed!"

Bianca simply rolled her eyes at Rachel and blew both lungs full of smoke in her direction, reminding Rachel of what she was too inept to do—smoke a cigarette.

Finally, Kelli stood up from the lawn chair and clicked the lighter twice until a flame appeared at the end of it. An appreciative Rachel leaned in toward Kelli and lit her cigarette. "You're gonna embarrass yourself for sure. You can't even work a lighter," Kelli hissed.

Bianca giggled joyfully at Rachel's shortcoming. What a delight to have the non-streetwise, church girl fall flat on her face.

"Don't worry about me," Rachel said to the two girls. "I'll have high school boys lighting my cigarettes."

"Like who?" Kelli wanted to know.

Silence fell between the three girls and Bianca waited to laugh at Rachel again. Bianca just knew she was bluffing. Rachel was trying to make herself seem more important than she actually was. Yet, before Bianca could conjure a laugh, Rachel finally spoke up.

"Like Darren Jenkins," Rachel said, with a wide grin across her face.

"That boy is in high school! You know goodness well he's not paying you a bit more attention than the man on the moon," Kelli squealed.

"That's not what he said last week when he French-kissed me at the church picnic."

"What?" Kelli and Bianca shouted in unison.

Now it was Rachel's turn to laugh at her friends. "You heard me! He used his tongue when he kissed me! I mean, I've kissed him a dozen times before, but last week he used his tongue!"

All three girls cackled like little hens. The laughter seemed to go on forever. It simply refused to end. Soon it took on a mind of its own. When it seemed the laughter would die, it found a way to tickle deep inside the girls' bellies to make it elevate to a higher level. The girls laughed until they thought their cheeks could not stretch any further.

Bianca's head ached from the laughter. Kelli laughed until she peed on herself, but she didn't dare tell her friends. Rachel laughed until she started to cough, which could had also been attributed to the thick cloud of cigarette smoke filling the garage.

After what seemed like half the night, when the laughter finally ended, in that awkward moment of silence Rachel asked, "Have you two babies ever kissed a boy?"

"Yeah, but you already know I have." Kelli continued, "I kissed Tommy Johnson, who lives across the street, in kindergarten and we got caught and the teacher told both of our mothers."

Bianca smiled at Kelli and sat in silence, embarrassed to tell of her single experience with kissing a boy. "Well, there was this one boy, Todd Simmons, in the fifth grade," she stammered. "It was more like Todd kissed me. Actually, I was standing there smiling and didn't get my pucker ready, so he kissed my teeth."

The contagious laughter returned. It went round and round again, tickling each girl's funny bone several times. Bianca's headache increased, Kelli let out a little more urine on the plastic seat and Rachel coughed some more.

This time when the giggles ended, Rachel asked, "And who's ever gone to second base?"

Bianca naively jumped right in and blurted, "Once I hit a homerun playing stick ball!"

When the contagious laughter struck again, it only infected Kelli and Rachel. And they laughed until it hurt.

Chapter 14
Kelli

In junior high school it seemed all the girls were budding like flowers in springtime—except Kelli. The other seventh and eighth-grade girls were running to the nurse's office for assistance with their periods. All of them seemed to be caught off guard; either needing a maxi pad for the unexpected flow or crying for an aspirin to deal with the cramps. However, Kelli, who was so well prepared and still carrying a purse around, couldn't catch a break. While the other girls developed curves in all the right places, breasts to fill out real bras, and butts and hips to fill out their pants Kelli grew straight up and down. The only thing enormous on Kelli were her feet. They seemed to grow at an alarming rate of speed.

Rita would say through her drunken haze, "If you grow to those feet, you'll be six feet tall!"

Kelli knew for sure she'd never get a boyfriend if that happened. She was already taller than most of the boys her age, most of whom had not yet hit their growth spurt. The nerdy glasses, coupled with her clown feet, were not helping Kelli blend into the crowd. Instead, she thought she stood out like a circus freak. Kelli cringed each time she looked into the mirror. Each day seemed to get worse; a new pimple, another blemish, and heck if she didn't just grow out of her favorite pink jelly sandals.

Somehow in the midst of her horrific adolescence, Kelli managed to establish herself as an honor student and an athlete. She was one of the stars of the girls' basketball team and was a force to be reckoned with on the track field. Her long legs and thin build had found a place to call home among her peers. Kelli may not have had the privilege of hanging out with the popular crowd like Rachel did, and she wasn't popular with the boys like Bianca was, but she had her own circle of friends that included the brainiacs and the jocks.

Kelli's position on the girls' basketball team turned about to be more beneficial than she could have imagined. As a member of the team, she practiced after school and in the neighborhood with some of the boys on the basketball team. Some of those boys were even taller than she and one in particular caught her eye. Eric Thomas, a tall, brown-skinned boy with crooked teeth, turned out to be not just a formidable competitor, but he also became her first puppy love and the boy with whom she would share her first real kiss.

As Kelli experienced the wonders and joy of first love, she was oblivious to what was going on around her. She had paid no attention to Rita's increasingly depressing mood and social withdrawal. Kelli had not noticed just how often Rita skipped work or even that she had been suspended from her job twice already. That is, until Rita's increased drunkenness demanded Kelli open her eyes to what was going on.

Kelli's awareness began one evening when she arrived home from school with a love note in her hand from her new beau. She was disheartened to find Rita had not gone to work. Much to Kelli's dismay, she was lying across the sofa in the front room, passed out in her own vomit, still holding onto a bottle of beer and surrounded by several others. Instead of going inside her bedroom and reading the note over again as she wanted to do, Kelli busied herself with taking care of Rita. She helped her mother from the sofa, assisted her in undressing and taking a shower. She wondered how many other girls her age had to be bothered seeing their mother naked, or wiping the puke from their face and chest. After getting Rita settled into bed shortly after four in the afternoon, Kelli scrubbed the rug and discarded all the beer bottles into the trash can on the back porch.

The routine became old abruptly. Kelli didn't mind Rita drinking a few beers. Usually Rita was a hoot when she was a little tipsy. She would laugh and make funny jokes. But once Rita had too much to drink, she became sad. Rita would sob and cry late into the night. Kelli, being a typical selfish teenager, was ill-equipped to assist her mother.

One evening after a late basketball practice, Kelli walked home from school exhausted. She was ready to jump into the shower and dive into the bed. As she rounded the corner of her neighborhood block, she noticed a familiar red car in the driveway. It was Ms. Tracy, her mother's best friend. Kelli loved Ms. Tracy and her two little twin daughters; Tonya and Sonya, but tonight she was in no mood for company.

The closer Kelli came to the house, the more the raised voices inside the dwelling could be heard. Soon Kelli could hear screams. Heart-wrenching, inconsolable, primal wailing shrieked through the crevices of the home and far down the street, until it filled Kelli's ears and caused her to panic.

Kelli instantly thought of Grammy. She and Rita had visited her grandmother the previous Sunday in the rest home and, once again,

Grammy appeared weaker than ever before. She wasn't able to hold her head up and could barely keep her eyes open throughout the visit. Still, it couldn't be. Kelli ran towards home with the additional weight of the heavy back pack she toted with her. The urgency of the situation made Kelli forget about the exhaustion which had consumed her only moments ago.

Kelli used the same fast speed as she did when running up and down the basketball court, to run home. Even so, it seemed to take an eternity for her to reach the front door of her house. As Kelli opened the door, she was met with the overwhelmingly familiar smell of alcohol. Certainly, Rita had been drinking heavily.

Ms. Tracy's eyes met Kelli's first. Tracy, with her large, round eyes set in her perfectly round, baby face, stared at Kelli in sheer horror as Kelli walked inside. Tracy was trying desperately to comfort Rita and repeated in a soothing voice, "It's gone be alright." Still, Rita yelled out of control, her face drenched with tears, eyes red and swollen.

Kelli ran to her mother's side, begging to know. "Rita, what's wrong?" she asked. She braced herself to hear the news of her grandmother's passing. Kelli knew deep down inside death was a natural part of life, but she was unprepared to let go of Grammy. She didn't want her grandmother to be gone.

Rita looked into Kelli's eyes for merely a second and simply responded, "Jackson," continuing to wail and cry with no abandon.

Then Kelli looked to Ms. Tracy for an answer. She wanted to know what had happened to her father. And she wondered, *Was he dead?* "What's wrong with Jackson?" Kelli asked desperately.

Ms. Tracy would not look Kelli in the eyes. Instead, she returned her attention to Rita, bringing her further into her embrace. Tracy rocked Rita as if she were an infant.

Kelli stood beside Ms. Tracy and Rita, not knowing what to do. Instinctively, Kelli's eyes welled with tears which created rivulets down her cheeks. Still, Kelli was determined to know what happened to Jackson. She looked to Ms. Tracy, who kept her eyes focused on Rita, still repeating the words, "It's gone be alright. I tell ya, it's gone be alright."

Kelli looked from Ms. Tracy to Rita and back to Ms. Tracy again. They were the adults. They were supposed to be in control and tell her, the child, what was going on. She sat mystified for several minutes and finally, she, too, wrapped her arms around Rita, crying right along with her mother. Something had happened to Jackson and whatever it was, it was bad. Otherwise, Rita would not be so upset.

It took what seemed like an eternity, but eventually Rita's screams quieted to sobs and then to whimpers. Rita had all but exhausted herself releasing her feelings of sorrow. Ms. Tracy helped Rita to lie down in her bedroom to rest. Kelli sat on the bare living room floor, missing her absent father. She had not seen him often, but now she feared she would not see him again. Not alive anyway.

"Kelli," Ms. Tracy said softly, stepping inside the living room. "I have to talk to you for a minute, Baby."

Kelli rose from the floor and sat on the edge of the sofa with her head down, focusing on the tattered rug underneath the cocktail table, while Ms. Tracy sat beside her.

"Is my daddy dead?" Kelli asked in a near whisper.

Ms. Tracy's eyes widened in surprise as she explained with a half grin, "No, Sweetheart. Your father isn't dead. That's not it at all."

Kelli looked up with some relief, coupled with some confusion written on her young face.

"Then why's Rita so upset, Ms. Tracy?"

Tracy sucked in a deep breath and blew it out decisively, before speaking. "This is going to be difficult for you to understand. You're just a child and this is a very adult situation. It's complicated and it's not pretty." Tracy took a long break before going on, licking her lips and wiping her forehead. "Look, Baby. This ain't easy for your mama and it ain't easy for me to tell you this, but" she stopped again, folding her hands in her lap, "but, your daddy left your mama."

"You mean they're getting divorced?" Kelli asked. She had friends whose parents had been divorced. The word was not foreign to her and right away she knew it would not be the end of her world. Heck, Jackson was practically never at home anyway. Her life would not change drastically.

"No, Sugar. They're not getting divorced. You see," Ms. Tracy paused, "they were never married to each other."

Kelli looked at Ms. Tracy, but never said a word. All she could think about was Jackson's driver's license, Jackson Carter who lived at 1524 Grant Circle. *Who was this man? s*he asked herself.

"Is Jackson really my father?" Kelli asked hesitantly, as a sinking feeling arose in the pit of her stomach.

"Yes, he's your daddy alright, but he's not married to your mama. Jackson is married to someone else," Tracy said holding her breath.

With her junior high school brain, Kelli tried desperately to wrap her mind around Ms. Tracy's words. She knew what marriage and divorce meant. But what did it mean that her father was married to another woman and not married to her mother? Now Jackson had left her mother.

"You mean I'm a bastard?" Kelli asked in shocked realization.

Tracy's big eyes bugged out and her nostrils flared. "Don't you ever let anybody call you that! Your mama wasn't married to your father, but you ain't nobody's bastard. Do you hear me?"

"Yes, Ms. Tracy," Kelli answered, holding her head down and then she began to cry. Not unrestrained like Rita, but still she cried. Ms. Tracy held the pre-teen in her arms like she, too, was an infant. Kelli recalled every memory of Jackson in those few minutes; every hug, every kiss and his deep dimples, which she had inherited. After blowing her nose and wiping her face, she concluded in her anger that she would have been better off if Jackson were dead.

When Kelli stopped sobbing, Ms. Tracy tucked her into bed and went home to her own family; a unit others might also say was complicated and ugly. She went home to her live-in boyfriend of six months and her five-year-old twin daughters.

Chapter 15
Rachel

Rachel had a blast in junior high school. She thought the boys were more mature, by leaps and bounds, than the silly boys in elementary school. There were more of them vying for her attention and more girls wanting to be just like her. Rachel was in heaven.

Fashion became Rachel's number one priority. She begged Mrs. Pettigrew to take her to the mall every weekend. And not just the lame Fairfield shops with their homely clothes, but to Dayton, Cincinnati and Columbus, where she could find the trendiest styles.

She bought every *Seventeen* and *Right On* magazine and tweaked her style to match that of the top celebrities. She was two steps ahead of all of the other girls in junior high and they envied her. Even some of Rachel's teachers attempted to replicate her style. Rachel became a real life, walking-talking billboard.

She learned to arch her thick eyebrows with a razor blade, apply lavender eye shadow as perfectly as the supermodels on the cover of *Vogue* and not be caught dead in last year's styles. It was as if Rachel had been born and bred in Beverly Hills instead of the miniscule Ohio town. Mrs. Pettigrew had undoubtedly created a fashion monster.

Rev. Pettigrew frowned at the amount of money the two spent each week, but his wife swore everything had been purchased on sale and she was not spending beyond their budget. However, Mrs. Pettigrew needed a bit more for her weekly allowance and some extra funds for "Rach," as she started to refer to her protégé.

Still, it made Rev. Pettigrew overwhelmingly proud when his wife and daughter stepped into the sanctuary each Sunday looking like a million bucks. His church may not have been the grandest, nor his house and car, but the two ladies in his life were spectacular in his eyes. Rachel rarely gave him any trouble at all, other than the normal pre-teen know-it-all attitude, and Mrs. Pettigrew served him well as a wife and first lady of the church.

Their life was nearly perfect, until one ordinary Sunday morning. The service had begun like so many others. The choir was in the spirit, the deacons were sitting in the front row and the ushers were standing at attention. The nurses dressed in their crisp white uniforms were equipped with a plethora of church fans for those who looked as if they would collapse from the stifling heat in the sanctuary. Mrs. Pettigrew sat on her designated second-row pew, and Rachel busied herself whispering with her cousins and passing notes. Yes, it was a typical Sunday all right.

That is, until a young woman dressed in a sharp pink suit, holding a pale shawl over her shoulders, entered the church, walked up the center aisle directly in front of the pulpit and stopped Rev. Pettigrew in mid-sentence. The amen corner stopped signifying, the organ player stopped his intermittent musical prelude and the church stood at attention, all just in time to hear the woman speak.

"Rev. Cleveland Pettigrew!" She shouted the pastor's name.

The good pastor stumbled over his words. He wanted to continue his sermon. He thought he could blink his eyes and make the woman go away. He tried, but it didn't work. The woman stood before him and the congregation, which also held his wife and daughter, demanding his attention.

Not swayed by the lack of his response, the woman bawled once more, "Rev. Cleveland Pettigrew!"

The Rev. did not respond, but motioned to the ushers to show her the way back to the door from whence she cometh.

"You want me to leave?" the woman asked the Rev. directly.

"Madame, please. This is the house of the Lord," Rev. Pettigrew reminded her, his typically virile voice quivering.

As the tallest and widest usher approached the woman, she bellowed, "But I need you to pray for my child." Suddenly, the woman raised up a tiny infant from beneath the shawl. The baby squirmed in his mother's hands and let out the sweetest coo one would ever want to hear. At the sight of the child, the enormous usher halted his forward motion.

Rev. Pettigrew stood shaking in the pulpit. He mumbled and fumbled and motioned his hand, as if shooing the woman away. The mighty usher resumed his movement towards the outspoken woman.

"But this is my only son, Pastor. I would like for you to say a special prayer for him," she continued, as the gigantic usher placed his hand on her forearm and began to direct the woman in pink toward the exit. "He needs a special prayer, Rev. Pettigrew," she continued as she back-pedaled towards the double church doors, accompanied by the massive usher. "He doesn't have a father," she called out. "This was an immaculate conception," she announced. As she neared the exit, the woman held onto the infant with one arm and grabbed hold of the church door with the other, making her final, begging plea. "This is God's child. Doesn't he deserve a prayer?" And then she was escorted out the door and vanished.

Rev. Pettigrew didn't miss a beat. He used the interruption to shift his sermon to the tricks of the devil. He advised his flock to be aware of Satan's presence in the church. He told them the evil one was the first to arrive at church and the last to leave. He said sometimes the devil walked right inside the sanctuary and interrupted the service. Before church ended, the entire congregation was feeling the spirit and doing the Holy Ghost dance.

Everyone, that is, except Ophelia Pettigrew. First Lady Pettigrew remained straight-faced, with her eyes set on her husband, the good preacher. She never nodded her head in agreement, or let out another "Amen" during the remainder of the service. Ophelia stood with her head held so high, her neck muscles strained to hold the position for the duration.

Most of the parishioners noticed Ophelia's stern posture, but none more than Rachel. She thought her mother acted quite peculiar following the strange episode, and she felt compelled to watch her mother's every move. She continued to watch Mrs. Pettigrew during their drive home from church. When Rachel began to talk about the strange turn of events, Mrs. Pettigrew flatly commented, "Yes, Rach. Like Rev. Pettigrew said, you have to be aware of the devil's presence in your home."

Rachel knew that wasn't what her father had said. He told them to be aware of the devil's presence in *the church*. Rachel noticed Mrs. Pettigrew had changed the words. She also noticed the single tear, which fell down her mother's cheek on the way home.

Chapter 16
Bianca

Bianca worked hard to become one of the beautiful people in junior high school by begging, borrowing and stealing—literally. For the first time in her life, the overall attention she received was beginning to turn positive. Suddenly, her biracial heritage was popular among her peers. It was cool to be mixed and she was one of very few mulatto kids in the area, so she stood out in a grand way.

After hearing Kelli talk about pressing out her kinky hair with a straightening comb, Bianca begged her best friend to teach her to do the same to her long, thick, curly mane.

"Kelli, you have to show me how to put a hot comb through my hair," Bianca nearly demanded.

"I guess your white mama don't know nothing about straightening your nappy head," Kelli giggled. "Come on in the kitchen, girl."

Bianca followed Kelli into the kitchen and watched her friend as she reached into a drawer and pulled out a comb with a fat black handle and metal teeth. Bianca was sure such a comb would only get tangled in her coarse hair. She watched as Kelli walked over to the stove and ignited the gas flame to one of the smaller burners. She then placed the metal teeth directly on the source of the heat. The two stared at the comb atop the stove fire.

"The key to pressing your hair is to get the comb hot, but not too hot. You don't want to burn your hair off. And you don't want to get the handle too greasy, or it'll slip right outta your hand and burn the crap out of your neck and back. You have to be careful around your edges and ears or you'll burn them, too. And the hardest part to do is your kitchen."

"Kitchen?" Bianca asked, puzzled.

"This part here in the back," Kelli said, lifting up Bianca's gigantic ponytail and placing her hand on the back of her hair near the neck, where the hair texture was extra tight and curly.

Bianca began to giggle, "That's a silly thing to call the back of your hair."

"It makes sense, actually. Rita always told me, if the kitchen in your house ain't in order, then your whole house looks a mess. But, if your kitchen is clean and polished, it makes your house look neat and clean. The same thing is true for the back of a black woman's hair," Kelli said, educating her half-white friend.

Bianca held perfectly still, as Kelli smeared grease on her hair and ran the hot comb through a large section of it. Bianca saw the smoke from the comb float through the air before her eyes, and she became extremely concerned. She hoped flames would not ignite in her hair, burning not only her edges and *kitchen*, but also her face. Kelli returned the comb to the fire on the stove to reheat it.

The smell of her own burning hair was repulsive to Bianca, but if the results were decent it would all be worth it. After the grease application and coaxing the hot comb through her hair was complete, Bianca ran into the bathroom to view the outcome. She looked into the mirror and saw herself transformed. Bianca had discovered for the first time in her life, what black women had known for many years; a pressing comb was a godsend!

Unlike Kelli's hair, which became straight, but stiff, after pressing, Bianca's hair was straight and bouncy. The next day at school, Bianca's hair was all the rave. The other kids thought it was chic. While Bianca's skin matched the light brown of a black person's, her hair was straight and flowing like a white girl's.

Once her hair issue was under control, Bianca was determined to improve her wardrobe. There was no way she could ask her mother to go traipsing off to the mall every weekend like the spoiled church girl, Rachel. It would be a cold day in hell before Mr. Goode gave up extra money to buy Bianca a pair of Jordache jeans. He barely had a word to say to her, since she had started her menstrual cycle. He stopped having sex with her, but he continued to mess with her; fondled her and said dirty things to her. Still, the last thing on his mind was giving up any money.

Bianca was able to coordinate some decent items from the Goodwill and a small five-and-dime store, but she desperately needed help in the wardrobe department. Kelli, who was taller than she, but the same size around, had outgrown several pairs of barely worn slacks and jeans. Bianca graciously accepted what were high-waters on Kelli, but fit perfectly on her body. It didn't hurt that Bianca developed curves in all the right places. She could make over a pair of Kelli's old jeans and a plain t-shirt into something hip and stylish by adding a wrist full of bangle bracelets and large earrings.

The last piece to Bianca's social success came when she went to the market with her mother. April Goode had gone into the grocery store and purchased two gallons of milk. She had, nevertheless, gotten away with stuffing a pack of pork chops inside her pocketbook and a box of rice under her coat. Bianca was nearly floored when it occurred to her that her mother had stolen those items from the store. When Bianca looked at her mother quizzically, April simply responded, "Mr. Goode's grocery money has to stretch. I don't get food stamps anymore."

Instantaneously, Bianca caught the stealing bug. She began to lift small items on occasion; a pack of Wrigley's chewing gum from the corner store and a small toy for Lilly from Kmart. It didn't take long for Bianca to expand her horizons. Soon she was pilfering everything she could get her hands on; clothing and jewelry from the finer department stores were her customary targets. She never worried about not having money to buy things she needed or wanted, she utilized her five-finger discount. Sure, April Goode noticed her daughter's accumulation of things, but she never spoke a word of it.

So, Bianca had it all together—or so she thought. After years of being teased and harassed for being biracial, she was now in fashion. She was getting attention from boys, and many of the girls wanted to look like her. They were all curious about her skin tone, hair texture and hazel-brown cat eyes. Many others thought Bianca was pretty. Soon Bianca, too, would be convinced of the same, and she would learn how to use her pretty face and curvaceous body as a weapon.

Chapter 17

Brick And Mortar

"Remember our kindergarten graduation?" Rachel asked Kelli, all too happy to exclude Bianca from the conversation as she had attempted all morning.

"It was the windiest day ever," Kelli replied. "Remember our graduation hats were flying all over the place?" Kelli giggled with fondness.

"I have a picture of Mrs. Pettigrew holding my cap, while the wind was blowing my white dress straight up in the air, showing off my little laced pink panties."

Bianca rolled her eyes at Rachel "And that was the last time you wore little panties, *Bertha Butt*," she retorted, causing Kelli to snicker.

"I wasn't talking to you, half-breed," Rachel shot back at Bianca. "It was me and Kelli's graduation, not yours. We've been together ever since, haven't we, Kelli?" Rachel and Kelli laughed together about the memory of their first graduation ceremony.

Now the girls, including Bianca, would share their eighth-grade graduation together. They had anticipated the ceremony for weeks, each girl talking excessively about what dress and shoes she would wear, how she would style her hair and who was assigned next to her in the seating arrangement.

The three junior misses chatted non-stop as they put the final touches to their ensembles in Rachel's bedroom. Each one was in a world of her own as they prepared for the most important day, thus far, in their young lives.

Kelli carefully pulled on a pair of flesh-toned panty hose, trying not to create a runner. However, the moment she moaned, "Daggone it!" the other girls knew exactly what had happened. Instinctively Rachel handed Kelli a bottle of clear nail polish from her dressing table. Kelli applied the polish generously to the tear in the hosiery located on her right thigh. Luckily, her dress would hide the tear, as long as the rip did not extend further down her leg.

Bianca removed pink sponge curlers from the front of her hair, which made it flip back into a Farah Fawcett fashion. She took great care in systematically combing what had become her crowning glory. Bianca left not a single hair out of place. She ended the daunting task by spraying a long stream of Alberto VO5 hair spray, ensuring her hair would not move, not even in a wind storm.

Rachel smeared on lip gloss and applied her signature lavender eye shadow. She even added mascara and eyebrow pencil to accentuate her eyes. Finally, she dusted her cheeks lightly with a warm chestnut blush to give the appearance of a healthy glow. She didn't want to look like a clown or one of the whorish women that Rev. Pettigrew complained wore too much rouge.

Once the three girls were dressed in their gold caps and gowns, they strutted off toward school; their friends and family would gather later. As the soon-to-be graduates approached the loud crowd of eighth-graders, Rachel remembered she forgot to stuff her bra with tissue. She began twisting her brassiere hoping to make her breasts stand out a bit more than they did naturally. "Just think. This'll be the last time we walk into this juvenile play pen. After today we will officially be high school girls!" Rachel squealed, sticking out her chest.

"Don't speak too fast. This group of eighth-grade babies is coming to high school right along with us. Unless a miracle happens this summer, we're gonna be stuck with the same group of immature idiots next year," Kelli explained, trying to bring Rachel down to ground level.

"But just think of all the upper classmen that'll be there. We won't even have to associate with freshmen boys next year," Rachel stated.

"Is that all you think about?" Bianca interjected. "Boys?"

"Of course not," Rachel said with a straight face and then burst into laughter.

The laughter bug infected each of the girls and they laughed nearly uncontrollably as they reached the crowd of graduates.

The ceremony was unremarkable. There were boring speeches and a solo sung off-key by a young girl; the valedictorian gave a less-than-inspiring address. The graduating girls and boys fidgeted in their seats and twisted and turned their caps and tassels excessively as sweat poured down their brows in the sweltering heat of the gymnasium. Inevitably, guests were asked to hold their applause to the very end of the long name of graduates called to receive their diplomas. Of course, the guests ignored the request and screamed and shouted, not just for joy, but because the end of the ceremony was nearing.

As the single-file line of junior high alumni poured out into the parking lot of the school gymnasium, the kids began to peel off the hot graduation robes. Blue and gold gowns hit the concrete and were trampled, while others were tied around necks and left blowing in the wind like Superman capes, with a few wrapped apron-fashioned around waists. Still, many garments were handed off to parents and siblings who were willing to carry them while the graduates busied themselves with the festivities.

Like most special occasions, parents scrambled to take their children's photos in the middle of the chaos, confusion and mayhem. The girls' graduation day would be no exception.

Ms. Tracy was at the ceremony with her twin daughters and Rita. Tracy took a picture of Kelli and her mother together, which showed the tall and lanky young girl with big feet and long arms wrapped tightly around Rita. They were all grateful Rita sobered adequately for the day of celebration. For a split second Kelli wished Jackson had been present. It was how she had dreamed her graduation picture would be, with her mother on one side, her father on the other.

Rev. Pettigrew took Rachel's and Mrs. Pettigrew's picture, both ladies the picture of perfection. Rachel stood with her back straight, flashing her picture-perfect smile. Her teeth had straightened nicely with braces. Rita came over and snapped a shot of Rachel with Rev. Pettigrew and Ophelia. Rita thought it was the neighborly thing to do.

April Goode took a photo of Bianca with little sisters Lily and Minnie. There had been no use in arguing with Mr. Goode about attending the graduation. April had dressed the girls and came without her husband and her sons.

It was Rev. Pettigrew's idea to take a picture of the three girls together; each one posing in their gold cap and gown, smiling and holding their eighth-grade graduation diploma high into the air for all to see. Now, the three girls would spend their high school years together.

Chapter 18
Kelli

An eighth-grader was the big man on campus in junior high, but a freshman in senior high school was considered something lower than dirt. To make matters worse, the upperclassmen referred to them as fresh meat instead of freshmen. The reference was degrading and made Kelli's skin crawl. Some of the boys had taken to giving specific names to the girls. Rachel was referred to as Big Butt Fresh Meat and she would hit any boy over the head with a heavy book who used the name. Bianca was known as Pretty Fresh Meat and she blushed each time she heard the words. Unsurprisingly, Kelli was called Skinny Fresh Meat and the name infuriated her. She would stick out her middle finger to the person who dared to call her the humiliating name.

As if she didn't have enough to worry about at home, lately, all Rita had been talking about each day was her new boss. Rita was certain he wanted to fire her. The man was never satisfied with Rita's performance. He watched her time away during the lunch hour like a hawk and rarely granted her days off. Lately he had been forcing Rita to work late and refused to pay her overtime. He thought it was bold of her to ask to be compensated for the things she should easily accomplish from nine to five, but had failed to do so. By the time she reached home late into the evening, Rita would immediately start recanting the events of the day, followed by an extensive episode of drinking.

One evening, setting two bottles of beer at the table while Kelli placed a Hungry Man TV dinner beside them, Rita vented, "And the worst part about the situation is he's a black man. You'd think a black man would cut his black employees some slack. Oh, no. He makes us work twice as hard as the white workers and doesn't pay us a dime of overtime."

"Maybe you should find a new job," Kelli offered sympathetically.

"It's not that easy," Rita schooled her daughter. "Jobs are hard to come by when you don't have any education. I barely made it out of high school, and only spent three months in secretarial school by the time I had you." Rita took a hearty swig of her first beer and wiped her mouth with the back of her hand. "Let this be a lesson to you, Kelli. Get your education before you start your family. Once you have bills to pay and mouths to feed, your options start drying up real quick." Rita continued swigging the brew.

Kelli glanced at her mother, who wasn't returning the look, and said under her breath, "I didn't ask to be born."

Without missing a beat, Rita placed her emptied beer bottle on the table, stared harshly at her daughter and responded, "But that don't stop you from asking for shit, now, does it?" she begged to know.

Kelli didn't respond, but pretended to engross herself in the fried chicken dinner.

Rita, too, began to satisfy her hunger with the chicken, mashed potatoes and carrots meal. The silence between the two grew thick. Finally, Rita looked up at Kelli and asked every kid's most dreaded question, "How was school today?"

"Fine," Kelli replied flatly, without even making eye contact with her mother.

Rita took a swig of her second bottle of brew and took in a deep breath before asking slowly, "I have to deal with a son-of-a-bitch all day at work and then come home and deal with an attitude from my own child, too?"

"I don't have an attitude," Kelli replied innocently and pretended to be shocked.

"Then, what's the matter?"

"It's just that Rachel's having a sleep-over Friday night and I'm not sure I wanna go."

"Is she inviting Bianca this time?" Rita wanted to know.

"Yes, Mrs. Pettigrew said she had to invite Bianca or she wouldn't allow Rachel to have the sleep over at all."

"Good for Ophelia. She's gotta keep a handle on that little brat. She can't decide she doesn't like somebody just because they're prettier than she is. Rachel Pettigrew will run into plenty of other girls in her life who are prettier than she is and she can't dislike 'em all or she won't have any friends."

Kelli sat silently as if in a trance listening to Rita rant.

"So why don't you wanna spend the night with your friends?"

Kelli did not open her mouth, but shrugged her shoulders.

"Is Rachel giving you a hard time, too?"

"No, it's not me she doesn't like, it's Bianca."

"Well, Rachel knows you and Bianca are competition. She doesn't stand to get all the attention from the boys when you two are around."

"I'm not prettier than Rachel," Kelli replied meekly.

"Oh, yes you are. Just look at your self some time good and hard in the mirror. You're beautiful." Rita said, grinning from ear to ear. "You're the spitting image of me when I was your age. And I had the boys buzzing around me, just like you'll have them swarming around you."

Kelli blushed in the presence of her mother. She never remembered feeling so embarrassed in front of Rita before. She teased, "It must be the beer talking."

"No, it's the God's honest truth," Rita said, as sure as she had been about anything in a very long time.

Cleaning up after dinner was easy. The trays from the TV dinners went into the trash bin, right along with Rita's empty beer bottles. The two forks, and one glass used for lemonade, were quickly washed out, dried and put away.

Right away Kelli locked herself into the bathroom and did just as Rita had suggested. She took a long look at herself in the mirror. The longer she looked, the more she became increasingly disappointed. No long and thick eyelashes like Rachel's appeared. Instead, Kelli thought she was the poster-child for starving waifs. Also, no hazel brown eyes like Bianca's appeared to make her face stand out. She thought she looked unremarkable. Her everyday, brown face was plagued with acne. Her common, brown eyes were a little bigger than what she thought they should be. Her nose, although not too broad, was also not quite slender.

Her lips were full, with a natural brown outline and pink toward the inside. She smiled at herself in hopes of a transformation. Her less-than-sparkling and far-from-straight teeth appeared, disheartening her once more. The only comfort she found were the dimples that appeared in both cheeks. The dimples were unique, not many others had such deep ones as she. Many people had even complimented her on the indentations, calling them cute. Still, those dimples had come from Jackson Carter and they made her sad when she looked at them.

Chapter 19
Rachel

It wasn't unusual for Ophelia to witness her daughter storm through the front door, run into her bedroom, slam the door behind her and stay locked inside, not coming out for dinner at all. Today, however, in the mere split second Ophelia was able to fix her eyes on her daughter, she saw Rachel had been crying. Ophelia hesitated, not looking forward to dealing with her hormonal teenage daughter. However, concerned for the well being of her only child she ventured toward Rachel's bedroom.

Hearing the soft knock at her door, Rachel managed to pull her body off her bed, where she had plopped only moments ago. She rose up, unlocked the door and dumped her body on the bed once more, muttering, never giving her mother permission to invade her personal space.

Ophelia opened the bedroom door and dared not enter, but asked from the safety of the doorway, "What's wrong, Rach?"

"My sleepover's going to be a disaster," Rachel whined in tears.

"Oh, Rach, don't be such a pessimist," Ophelia scolded her daughter as she entered the bedroom and sat down on the bed. "Come on, tell Mother what's the matter."

Rachel sat up on the bed, wiping the tears away with her shirt sleeve, "You just don't understand."

"Rachel, I know it seems to you like I was a high school girl a million years ago, but for me it only seems like yesterday. I remember how difficult high school was. I remember the uncertain feelings, wanting to fit in, yet wanting to stand out." Ophelia thought for a moment about mentioning boys, but she hoped she could reserve that frank discussion until her daughter's senior year. "I especially remember how the others girls could be so mean."

Rachel looked up at her mother, surprised, because the girls were exactly the problem. "How did you know it was the girls?"

"The names and faces may change, but everything else remains the same, Rachel. You're in your first year of high school, the time when cliques and groups are formed. Everyone's clamoring to find their place in the social groups and are willing to do nearly anything to hold their position. That's where the meanness comes in."

Rachel sniffed twice before explaining, "Two of the popular girls said I'm stuck up, because I'm Rev. Pettigrew's daughter. They said they won't come to my party, and started telling the other invited girls not to come either, so some of them aren't coming now."

"Honey, don't let things that aren't true upset you. You are Rev. Pettigrew's daughter and this entire community has picked and probed into this family for years. You're no stranger to their attention. Just take it all with a grain of salt. It's the only way to get through it."

"But what am I going to do now? I only have four girls coming to my sleep over; Tracy and Penny in my homeroom, Kelli and Bianca. I'll be the laughing stock of the whole school," Rachel explained, with tears resuming.

"That's an easy solution," Ophelia calmly stated. "Just invite a couple of your cousins over. How about your Uncle Robert's daughter, Shelly? She's a cheerleader for the varsity team at her school."

"Shelly barely even speaks to me at church. Do you really think she'll come to my party?"

"Don't worry about that. I'll call your Uncle Robert myself and tell him his brother, Rev. Pettigrew, insists she come to the party."

Rachel reached over and hugged her mother, "Mrs. Pettigrew, that's a great idea! And I'll invite Aunt Rhonda's daughters, Angie and Vanessa. They're both Barbizon models."

"And I'd better call and remind Rhonda how her brother's church paid her utilities before she married that second husband of hers with all the money."

"When the other girls who turned my party down find out about my cousins coming over, they'll be sorry!"

Ophelia didn't know if she wanted to tell Rachel, *That's the spirit!* or *That's not the right attitude to have*. She was just so grateful the crisis was over. "Well, I'd better get on the phone and call your aunt and uncle. Your party's in two days and I don't have much time left."

Rachel could hardly wait for school the next day to let her friends know who would be joining them for her sleepover. She was so excited a perfect plan had been placed into motion. When she couldn't reach Kelli that evening, she called Bianca to share the good news. After all, Rachel thought, her cousins were even prettier than Bianca and she wanted Bianca to know it.

Chapter 20
Bianca

It was her first kiss with Dion Wright and it happened under the bleachers on the football field after school. Bianca was taken by surprise at just how fast her hear beat. She hoped Dion couldn't feel it through their jackets, his sweatshirt and her cotton blouse, but she was sure he could. Bianca could feel her body heat up as the intensity of their kiss ignited flames deep inside her. With the exception of her legs, which were bare and hanging from under her mini skirt, she felt as if it were the middle of July instead of a brisk autumn afternoon.

Bianca tried to relax and play it cool, but her body was tight and rigid. Her back was pressed straight against a metal pole and she wanted to shift her weight from her right leg to her left, but that was nearly impossible to do with Dion's tongue thrust in her mouth. She wasn't even sure when to take in a breath. Her breathing was labored and she was certain Dion would notice this tale-tale sign of a novice kisser. She had bragged about being experienced, but in reality, all she knew about was the torture of being raped.

Dion moved closer and closer to her until she felt herself pinned against the pole, it becoming a part of her, straightening her back fully upright. She supposed Dion knew what he was doing since he was a sophomore and said he had taken girls under the bleachers before. She hoped their trip was a special one and that he intended to take no other girls to their spot after that day.

Without warning, Bianca felt Dion's hands move from her waist, down to her hips and then to her butt. He seemed to hold onto her for dear life and it seemed only appropriate she do the same in return. While Bianca's arms had been draped loosely around Dion's neck, she now wrapped them tightly around his waist and gripped him with young passion. His groin increasingly pressed firmly into hers.

After some time, Bianca thought she was as comfortable as one could get pressed against a metal pole. That is, until Dion changed the game. His right hand, which had been gripping and rubbing her behind, slid under her blouse and he began to fondle her breast through her bra. His touch made her uncomfortable, as flashes of Mr. Goode on top of her came to the forefront of her mind.

Without warning, Dion's hand moved from her breasts and slid under her miniskirt. Quickly he maneuvered her panties aside and his finger entered her vagina. Bianca was well into her secret place where she had escaped so many times before when her body was being invaded. It was if she were a ghost looking down on an innocent girl being violated once more.

Chapter 21

An Unfinished Basement

After changing into their best pajamas, the girls gathered on a large rug in the Pettigrew basement with blankets and pillows tossed about. Rachel looked at her guests and was satisfied with those in attendance. She would definitely have bragging rights when she returned to school on Monday. Mrs. Pettigrew had fed the girls pizza and they had watched the ABC Friday night movie of the week. Now they would stay up laughing and giggling for hours playing Truth or Dare.

A few rounds of the juvenile game accomplished all the silly dares, the juvenile ones like making calls on the telephone and asking strangers if their refrigerator was running, waiting for the expected "Yes," and shouting with shrieks of laughter, "Better go catch it!" Swallowing ice, holding their breath for thirty seconds, and showing off their birth marks had been done over and over again when the game began to get stale.

Finally, Shelley, Rachel's cousin, declared, "From now on, no more choosing Dare. You have to pick Truth."

For a moment, Rachel was taken aback; after all it was her party. However, since Shelley was a cheerleader on the varsity team at her school, Rachel let her cousin slide this one time. "Yeah, you can only pick Truth," Rachel chimed in weakly. Next, Rachel looked at one of her homeroom classmates and asked, "Tiffany, Truth or Dare?"

Tiffany, a girl popular for a beautiful singing voice in the school choir, yet who was not quite special to look at, came to attention and replied, "Truth," as it had been established to be her only choice.

Rachel thought for a moment before asking, "Tell us your all-time embarrassing moment?"

Tiffany thought briefly and then responded, "One day last week I had dressed in a hurry for school and when I sat down in homeroom, Anthony Hayes pointed at my socks and screamed out, 'Tiffany has on mismatched socks!' I looked down and found out I was wearing one black and one blue sock!"

Kelli and Bianca giggled and the other girls stared at them blankly. Finally, Shelly blurted out, "These are baby questions." Rachel wanted to let out a giggle, but held back since the other girls did not find Tiffany's incident to be funny.

Rachel moved on and asked her cousin, "Angie, Truth or Dare?"

Angie, a pretty, brown-skinned girl, but not very smart, replied, "Dare."

Rachel became frustrated, "You have to pick Truth."

Angie put her head down in embarrassment, "Oh, I meant Truth."

Rachel rolled her eyes and sighed heavily before she asked, "When did you first come on your period?"

"Sometime during the night. I woke up and blood was all over my sheets," Angie said matter-of-factly.

"No, stupid, how old were you?" Shelly barked.

"The sixth grade," Angie said proudly.

"Me, too," Rachel remarked, as if it gave Angie a stamp of approval.

Rachel then asked her next cousin, "Vanessa, Truth or Dare?"

Vanessa, who was bored, flatly replied, "Truth."

Rachel opened her mouth, but Shelly beat her to the punch by nearly demanding to know, "How far have you ever gone with a boy?"

The question made Vanessa perk up. She hesitated and thought about her answer. She had gone all the way several times with several different boys, but this group of girls didn't need to know that. She whispered, "My boyfriend in the tenth grade laid on top of me on the couch and grinded me."

All the girls snickered and laughed in unison. Some laughed because they had gone further and others because they still waited in anticipation to go that far with a boy.

The excitement hyped Rachel and she was ready to hear more. She nearly screamed out, "Penny, Truth or Dare?"

Penny said, "Truth" and hoped she wasn't asked the same question. Although Penny was in Rachel's homeroom, she had been held back twice and academics weren't the only thing she was slow in. Penny didn't have any experience with boys at all. She was still hoping for her first kiss.

Rachel asked the question as if she had come up with it all on her own, "How far have you gone with a boy?"

Penny thought about her older sister, Paris, and what she had heard Paris talking about on the telephone when she said, "At the movie theatre, I let this boy put his hand inside my bra."

Again, more hooting and hollering occurred.

Rachel was feeding on the excitement and rushed on. "Bianca, Truth or Dare?'

Bianca tried to keep her confidence and answered, "Truth." Yet, all the while inside she feared telling the truth. It had just happened that day under the bleachers and maybe it was nobody's business but her own. Besides, could she really trust anyone in this room, aside from Kelli? Yet, some of the girls were still grinning from the excitement of the game and who was she to be a kill joy? Why not keep the fun going and just tell the truth?

"How far have you gone with a boy?" Rachel asked, grinning.

Suddenly it seemed harmless to tell, so Bianca threw caution to the wind, "Today Dion fingered me under the bleachers after school."

The other girls laughed, except for Rachel, whose mouth stood wide open. She yelled, "Bianca, you're just a big ol' ho!"

Bianca froze and just sat there with her mouth open. She wanted to respond, but the words did not come to her brain. Thankfully, Kelli was right beside her and she jumped right in.

"Shut up! Don't you call her a ho!" she yelled. "You're a hypocrite, Rachel. You've been running around here sticking your tongue down every boy's throat who'll let you and you have the nerve to call Bianca a ho?"

Shelley interjected, "Well, it is kinda nasty to let a boy finger you," she said accusingly.

"And you shut up, too!" Kelli cut Shelly off quickly.

Rachel rose to her feet and insisted, "Kelli, nobody was even talking to you!"

Kelli also rose to her feet, ready to go toe-to-toe with the girl she had been friends with since they were babies, and responded harshly, "Well, I'm talking to you."

Loud footsteps resounded throughout the basement and Rev. Pettigrew appeared, clothed in his pajamas, a heavy housecoat and slippers. "What's going on down here?" He demanded to know.

Rachel turned to look at her father. She wondered if she should tell him about their game of Truth or Dare, and how Bianca had just revealed herself to be a 'ho,' or if that would only spark Kelli to tell her father she had been tongue-kissing boys left and right.

"Nothing, Rev. Pettigrew. We were just about to go to bed."

Kelli grabbed her blanket, pillow and bag and said, "I was just leaving, Rev. Pettigrew."

Bianca found her voice and said, "And I'm leaving, too." She snatched her belongings and headed for the front door behind Kelli.

Chapter 22
Kelli

It began to drizzle as Bianca and Kelli headed across Rev. Pettigrew's precisely manicured lawn. Kelli didn't own any slippers so her feet were soaked as she stamped furiously across the grass. Bianca's march matched that of her comrade's while her house slippers made a flip-flopping sound as she moved swiftly across the wet yard. As Kelli reached her front door, she searched inside her overnight bag for the door key, while Bianca stood silently with her head hanging low. As Kelli looked at her friend's face with the aid of only the moonlight, she could see Bianca's face soaked with tears. Kelli was too mad to cry. Instead, she wanted to punch somebody. And she would have punched Rachel if Rev. Pettigrew had not come downstairs to the basement in the knick of time to save Rachel's big behind from a butt whipping.

"Are you coming in?" Kelli asked angrily. Not angry with Bianca, but Rachel.

"Yeah, why not," Bianca replied. "I got permission to sleep over. I might as well sleep here."

Kelli found the key, entered the front door and readily dumped her sleeping bag, pillow and overnight bag on the floor. Bianca followed suit. Kelli turned on the television, keeping the volume low, in order not to awaken Rita, and plopped down on the sofa with Bianca dropping down beside her. Both of their minds were still spinning from the fiasco that had just happened next door with the Wicked Witch of the West and her Flying Monkeys.

Whispering, Kelli said softly, "I swear this is it; I'm not friends with Rachel after this. She acted so self-righteous tonight, always showing off in front of other people. She had no business calling you a name like that." Kelli turned to face Bianca. "That was just wrong."

Bianca sat starring at the TV. "Rachel's a bitch," she stated softly and plainly.

"Yeah, she's a bitch," Kelli agreed. "She's a jealous bitch."

Bianca used her pajama top to dry the tears from her face. "That doesn't make any sense. Rachel doesn't have anything to be jealous of. She has everything. A mother and a father. A whole church that worships the ground she walks on and she gets everything she wants. She doesn't have a reason to be jealous about anything."

"She's jealous because you're prettier than her," Kelli revealed.

"Well, she's stupid. I don't have half the stuff she has. Besides, boys like her, too."

"Yeah, but she wants to look like you. She wants to be light-skinned, with light eyes and a cute figure. Not that big *Bertha Butt* of hers."

The girls giggled in hushed tones for just a moment and the tension release felt good to both of them, but immediately Bianca started to cry again.

Kelli walked into the kitchen and brought Bianca some napkins to wipe her face.

"Here," she said, "don't cry," wanting to offer her friend some sympathy, but with her anger standing in the way.

Bianca sniffed a few more times and tried hard to make the tears stop. She could not stop them, but at least they began to slow down. The girls sat in silence staring at the television for a long time. Kelli was steaming inside at how badly Rachel could treat another human being. Bianca was feeling embarrassed, hurt and angry about sharing something so personal in a room nearly full of strangers.

Finally, Kelli broke the silence with a bright idea that popped inside her head. "Bianca, let's finish playing the game."

Bianca sniffled, "What are you talking about?"

"I'm talking about you and me playing Truth or Dare?"

"The two of us?"

"Yes, the two of us," Kelli said, looking intently at Bianca. "Trust me."

After what had just occurred that evening, Bianca was certain Kelli was worthy of her trust. Kelli had stood up for her in a basement full of girls who had made fun of her.

"Okay," Bianca said hesitantly. She cleared her throat and asked, "Kelli, Truth or Dare?"

"Truth," Kelli replied calmly.

"I don't know what to ask," Bianca confessed.

"Ask me what my secret is."

"Okay, Kelli, what's your secret?"

Kelli took in a deep breath. She knew Bianca deserved some honesty in return tonight. "My mother and father were never married." Kelli's heart began to ache from saying the words out loud for the first time. "I thought they were married, until last year when I found out my father is married to someone else. His last name is Carter. The only way I know that is because I saw his driver's license." Kelli paused. "He left my mother last year. She's been getting drunk really bad ever sense. I haven't seen him or heard from him and he lives right here in Fairfield at 1524 Grant Circle." Kelli's head hung low and tears began to fall. Now, Bianca handed her a napkin.

"My turn," Bianca said softly.

Through tears Kelli asked, "Bianca, Truth or Dare?"

"Truth," Bianca replied meekly.

"What's your secret?"

"My stepfather's molested me since I was seven years old. I never told my mother. He stopped having sex with me when I came on my period. He hates me. He calls me Lilly's mammy and my own mother doesn't do anything about it. I've never seen my real father before. I don't even know his name; my mother won't tell me." Bianca broke down sobbing.

Kelli sat in silence thinking Rachel and her stupid friends may have started the silly game of Truth and Dare, but she had ended it. Together she and Bianca had sealed their relationship that night. They were friends through and through now. They had bore their souls to one another and the event did not end in finger pointing and laughing. From that day forward the game of Truth or Dare would become an important part of their friendship.

Chapter 23
Rachel

An entire week passed before Ophelia Pettigrew questioned Rachel about her missing-in-action best friend, Kelli Brown. Kelli had not called, come to visit or joined the family for dinner on a single occasion for an entire week. In fact, Rachel had walked to school alone all week. Rachel shrugged off her mother's concern. A second week passed before the loneliness crept inside Rachel's heart. A week without Kelli, she could stand, but two weeks was even too much for her.

Rachel knew what she had to do to make amends. It would be a lot more difficult than just apologizing to Kelli. That alone would be simple. She and Kelli had been friends forever. Painstakingly, Rachel knew she was going to have to apologize to Bianca as well. That part would be a bit more complicated. She didn't care that much for Bianca and she truly wasn't sorry for calling her a *ho*. What kind of girl let boys do nasty things to them like that and under the school bleachers? She wasn't sorry at all.

Still, Rachel missed Kelli. There was no dodging this one. She would have to take one for the team. Rachel prepared herself mentally for the challenge during the morning of the next school day. She plotted and planned her approach until she came up with the best laid scheme. It would take timing and possibly some groveling, but success was within her grasp.

It was after lunch when Rachel walked right up to Bianca's locker in the middle of passing period. Bianca greeted her with a frown and Rachel tried real hard to overlook it.

"Hey, Bianca, I was hoping I'd find you here," Rachel said almost sweetly.

"Why, did you have some more names to call me?" Bianca asked, twisting her neck. She was becoming a real black girl indeed.

Some of the passersby slowed their pace, not sure if the exchange would turn into a girl-fight complete with scratching and pulling hair. No one wanted to give up a ring side seat.

Rachel smiled, reassuring herself, Bianca and everyone around that this was a friendly discussion. She would bite her tongue until it bled if necessary. "No. I actually came to apologize," Rachel said gritting her teeth.

Bianca's demeanor softened, but she remained on guard. It had been a long two weeks with rumors of her being a *ho* floating around the school. Dion Wright had dropped her like a hot potato after he confirmed the rumors to be true within his circle of friends, igniting the rumors even more. If it had not been for Kelli talking and standing by her side, Bianca would not have been able to show her face in school. "You apologizing to me? Get real."

"I'm serious," Rachel said with a long sigh. "Look, I was wrong. I had no business calling you names and I'm just saying I'm sorry. Okay?"

Bianca slammed her locker door shut in defiance. She didn't want to let Rachel off the hook so easily, but she desperately needed a friend. Rachel, with all her flaws, wasn't so bad all the time. "I don't know, Rachel."

"Do you want to walk home from school together?" Rachel offered.

Bianca looked down at her feet and replied, "I was going to wait for Kelli after basketball practice."

"Well, good, I'll meet you back at your locker and we'll wait for Kelli together," Rachel said and walked away without even giving Bianca a chance to reply. That would be perfect. Once

Kelli saw with her own two eyes that Rachel had made up with Bianca, Kelli would be sure to fall in step. Perfect.

Chapter 24
Bianca

Being friends with both Kelli and Rachel was remarkable. Bianca thought they were quite a threesome. She was no longer the third wheel when Rachel and Kelli were hanging out, but she had become an equal. There were even times when just she and Rachel hung out together or walked home from school, just the two of them. Bianca joined the Pettigrews for dinner on occasion and was even invited to their church spring revival.

April and Mr. Goode had just gotten used to Kelli, with her brown skin and soft demeanor, knocking on their door, but Rachel, with her brilliant dark skin, blew their minds. Rachel was outspoken and her strength clearly upset Mr. Goode internally when Rachel entered his house.

Yet, even Mr. Goode feared God enough not to talk about the daughter of Rev. Pettigrew forthrightly. Oh, he huffed and puffed under his breath, but he never said a cross word to Rachel.

"Do you like him?" Rachel asked Bianca of her stepfather as the two aimlessly stared at stolen copies of Vogue magazine.

Bianca was careful to speak low, although Mr. Goode was not yet home from work. Still, she didn't want Mr. Goode's children overhearing her reply. "He's okay, I guess, for a step-father," Bianca replied as she flipped the page of the periodical in her hand.

"I think he looks at me funny. Does he ever look at you funny?" Rachel said and searched Bianca's face for the truth.

Bianca set the magazine down for only a quick second as she responded, "Yeah, he looks at you funny. You're the darkest thing that's ever stepped foot in his house."

"Your other side of the family never comes over to visit you?"

Bianca put the Vogue magazine down again and sighed heavily, "I don't have another side of my family. There was my black father who got my mother pregnant and that was it. There are no grandparents, aunties, uncles or cousins. There's not even a black father anymore. I've never seen him."

"How could you have never seen your father?"

Bianca was getting tired of her line of questioning. She had told Rachel this over and over again. "Look, Rachel, that's just it. I've never met my father before. My mother's never told me anything about him. I don't even know his name?"

"Well, that's just silly. How could you not know your own father's name," Rachel exclaimed, nearly scolded her.

It was times likes this that Bianca questioned if Rachel was truly her friend. Kelli had never seemed to badger Bianca like this. Frustrated, Bianca replied, "Rachel, drop it. I said I don't know anything about him and I don't." The hurt was beginning to well up in Bianca's chest. A girl could take the shame of not knowing who her father was for only so long.

Rachel sat back and returned to flipping pages again, and Bianca soon relaxed and fell in suit. However, like clock work, Rachel's mind returned to her previous course of thought, when she blurted, "Have you ever seen your birth certificate? Your father's name would have to be on that."

Bianca looked up at Rachel and as annoying as Rachel was, she was right. Her father's name had to be on her birth certificate. Bianca sat up straight and thought about it for a moment. Then it struck her her mother kept all of the family's important papers locked in a small chest on the highest shelf of her closet. She kept the key to the chest in the top drawer of her chest of drawers.

While Rachel acted as the look out, Bianca slipped into her mother's bedroom and retrieved the small brown box and the key to the chest. She knew she had to move quickly; one of her brothers or sisters could come up the steps at any moment. Bianca searched the box and found an array of documents, most of which did not make any sense to her. But there was a rental agreement for the house they lived in, a car title for the broken down piece of junk they drove and a marriage license for April and Mr. Goode. Although it was not what she was looking for, she pulled out the marriage license and read it. There, in black and white, she saw where April Scott and John Goode had applied for a marriage license. Rachel stared at the document, frozen in place; her brow frowned deeply and her mouth dropped open.

Rachel snatched the document from Bianca's hands and read it over, but she saw nothing alarming. She saw April's name and she knew that was Bianca's mother, and she saw John's name and knew that was Mr. Goode. Yet, what Rachel didn't know was that Bianca called April's parents Grandma and Grandpa Miller. Somewhere between her birth and her marriage certificate, April's surname had changed to Scott.

Chapter 25

Behind Closed Doors

It was another Friday night spent together in Rachel's bedroom. All three girls huddled together sharing the excitement of the school week. Kelli talked excessively about a junior named Kevin, whom she had a crush on. Bianca was particularly quiet that evening and Rachel pretended to pay attention as she focused more on painting her toenails fire-engine red.

"I think Kevin's got the coolest school jacket of all the varsity players. He's lettered in basketball, track and football. Plus he'll be captain of the basketball team this year. I want to letter in basketball and track this year, so my jacket'll be cool like his. Well, in a girl kind of way, anyway," Kelli chatted on until she was interrupted by a soft knock at Rachel's bedroom door.

Rachel sprang to her feet, yet careful not to ruin her fresh pedicure and opened the door to her mother. “Yes, Mrs. Pettigrew?”

Her mother was dressed in her night clothes and even had her hair in curlers with a thin pink scarf wrapped around her head, “Sweetheart, would you girls like to come join me in my bedroom for the Friday night movie of the week?”

“No, thanks. I think we’ll just hang out in here and get some homework done.” Rachel knew they wouldn’t start their homework tonight. Rachel knew she would wait until Sunday evening as she always did.

“Okay. Your father will be having some gentlemen coming over tonight from the church. They’ll be in the living room and I don’t want you girls to get in their way.”

“We’ll stay in my room,” Rachel promised. “And I’ll keep my door closed to keep out the cigar smoke,” Rachel chuckled.

“And keep your ears closed to keep out the trash talk,” Ophelia said, making herself laugh.

Rachel smiled and shut her bedroom door to return to her friends. She repositioned herself to place the final coat of polish on her toes. Rachel hurriedly took over the conversation before Kelli could return to her boring discussion of Kevin, with his buck teeth and big nose, whom Rachel couldn’t care less about. “Okay, you didn’t hear this from me," Rachel started, which was the signal for the others to listen up. "But I heard," she paused, "that Kerri Dickson is pregnant!"

The others gasped in unison! "By who?" Kelli blurted out.

Rachel grinned, "You won't believe this." She let Kelli and Bianca hang onto her every word. She took her time formulating her words, "But I heard she's pregnant by a teacher!"

Again they gasped! Bianca scoots in closer to Rachel to make sure she hears the entire story clearly. "That's crazy. How could she mess around with a teacher?"

"I bet it's that slimy Mr. West," Kelli adds, "He's always undressing girls with his eyes. Yesterday I was walking down the hall and when a girl with a tight skirt and big fat booty walked past, he actually stopped, turned around and watched her booty shake as she walked away. He's nasty!"

Laughter boomed throughout the room.

"No, it's not Mr. West," Rachel said, determined to make her friends guess again.

"Is it Miss Howe, the gym teacher?"

That made them all laugh again.

"No, silly," Rachel said, still recovering from laughter. "Remember that real young math substitute teacher at the beginning of the year?"

"The one that graduated from Ohio State?" Kelli asked. He had substituted for her math teacher.

"That's the one," Rachel said. "Mr. Gold, he's the one that got Kerri pregnant."

"But he's only about five feet tall and Kerri's one of the tallest girls in school," Kelli protested.

Bianca responded, "I don't think his height had anything to do with it."

They giggled. "He still lived at home with his parents, right next door to Kerri and she was sneaking in his bedroom window every night, they said. When she told Mr. Gold she was pregnant he moved out from his parents' house and stopped teaching the next day!"

"That's dogged," Bianca added. "He did her dirty."

The girls commiserated over Kerri Dickson's pregnant state and shared the rest of the school gossip before they parted company for the night, leaving Rachel alone in her bedroom to experience the solitude only a teenage girl could know. She used clear polish on her fingernails. She knew Rev. Pettigrew would not tolerate the hot red polish on her fingernails. Heck, he wouldn't even permit her to date until she turned 16. At 15 years and 6 months the wait seemed like an eternity. So, Rachel busied herself with her manicure and how she wished she had a television in her bedroom until the door bell rang.

One by one, Rev. Pettigrew's cronies arrived. Rachel sat on the top step of the staircase and waved to her two uncles, one of the deacons from the church and one of her father's old classmates from 1960 something. The men slapped backs and gave each other the high five. When one of the uncles pulled out a bottle from a brown paper sack and broke the seal on it, immediately Rev. Pettigrew shooed Rachel to her bedroom. It was officially time for the *trash talking* that Mrs. Pettigrew had spoken of.

Soon after, Rachel changed into her pajamas and rolled her hair in curlers, similar to how her mother had hers. She then returned to painting her toe nails a bright glossy red her father would not see those. Still, boredom did not escape her. She had been asking her parents for a TV in her room, but once again, their stupid rules had stood in the way of her happiness. She flipped through a few magazines and then it dawned on her, the noise on the first floor had subsided. She could still hear the men, but the noise was muffled. They had either gone outside to the back porch or down into the basement. Suddenly, Rachel was thirsty and she needed a drink of water from the kitchen. She grabbed her housecoat and tiptoed down the steps. Once she reached the bottom of the staircase, she could tell that the muffled voices were coming from the basement, but there weren't just voices, there was laughter. She wondered what was so funny. The door to the basement was closed and she tiptoed to it and cracked the door open just slightly. She could hear someone talking and then all the men laughing. She waited for the laughter to stop and the one talking spoke again. The voice was coming from the old record player in the basement. It made a slight scratching sound as the storyteller continued. The men all laughed again. Whoever the man on the recording was swore like a sailor. Rachel covered her mouth at the shock of the long line of swear words and she covered her mouth again to stifle a laugh. She stood next to the basement door for nearly ten minutes until the final joke was told and the men shared their final group laughter. Rachel tiptoed back up the steps, still giggling softly. It would be years before she knew the voice of the jokester to be that of Richard Pryor.

Chapter 26
Kelli

It was a typical Saturday morning and Kelli found herself in the kitchen alone preparing breakfast. As bacon sizzled in the cast iron skillet, she scrambled eggs in a bowl. She flipped the bacon once and was reaching for a loaf of wheat bread, when she heard stirring in the hallway outside Rita's bedroom door. It was hours before noon and she could hardly believe Rita was moving around so early. Maybe Rita would join her for breakfast if she was not hung over.

Footsteps approached the kitchen and without turning around, Kelli asked, "Want some breakfast?"

A strong masculine voice replied, "No, but thanks anyway." His reply came out just as smoothly as if he responded to Kelli every day, but the voice was unfamiliar.

Kelli whipped her body around from the stove and faced the male stranger. He was an impressive man—dark as the midnight sky and gigantic. It was the first time Kelli could recall Rita had brought another man into the house besides Jackson. Caught off guard, Kelli stood in place, embarrassed to be wearing a thin worn nightgown she had long ago outgrown. Only the kitchen counter top separated her from an unknown, full-grown man. Her facial expression must have spoken volumes, because the stranger took a step back in response.

Holding both hands into the air, as if he were a hostage, the stranger explained, "I didn't mean to startle you. You must've thought I was your mother."

"Yeah, where is she?" Kelli asked cautiously, looking the stranger up and down, which was no easy feat.

"She's still in the bed asleep," he replied gently.

"And who are you?" Kelli asked with a raised eyebrow.

"I'm a friend of your mother's," the stranger said confidently.

He stood before Kelli in wrinkled black slacks and a grey silk shirt, with the wide collar landing on the tip of his shoulder. His eyes were large and bugged out. Yet, his expensive leather shoes and shiny watch made up for them. Kelli could hardly believe the massive man standing before her. She wondered where Rita had found him and how in the world he had even fit through the front door.

"What kind of friend are you?" Kelli asked curiously.

"Actually your mother and I work together," he said matter-of-factly. "I'm Able Taylor," he announced, tipping an imaginary hat and grinning, exposing a wide gap between his two front teeth.

"That's funny. She's never mentioned you, Able."

"Well, that hurts right here," Able teased, holding his hand over his heart. Acting as though he had been offered it, Able took a step over to the small dining room table and took a seat. His large frame made the chair look to be doll furniture.

Kelli giggled as she flipped the bacon frying on the stove. Able, who had too much to drink the night before, felt queasy at the sight and smell of food. Yet, he managed to silently hold back a forcible gag deep inside his throat.

"Don't feel bad," Kelli cautioned Able, "Rita doesn't talk about anyone at work accept her boss. She hates his guts!"

Able's eyes widened. "Oh, is that so?" he commented, bidding Kelli to tell more.

"Yeah, she complains about him every day when she comes home from work. She says he's a real S.O.B." Kelli hoped to impress Able by talking like an adult. When she looked into Able's eyes, she was sure she had made an impression.

Able Taylor stood with his mouth agape. "Wow, I had no idea."

"Well, what do you think of him?" Kelli asked.

Able stammered and stuttered for a few moments. "Well, I…I think the boss is a pretty cool cat. He's a hard worker and I think most of the employees enjoy working for him."

"That's not what Rita says," Kelli added, removing the bacon from the skillet and pouring eggs inside. "You must be working for a different boss, because Rita said the whole office would just as soon kill him as look at him. They all hate his guts."

Able began to break out in a sweat. He could hardly believe what he was hearing besides, he was hearing it from Rita's daughter! He had just been intimate with Rita a few short hours ago.

"Those are pretty strong words," Able commented. "It sounds like they're being too hard on the boss. Really, no one could be that horrible."

Kelli nodded in the affirmative and revealed, "They're Rita's words, not mine. I'm just telling you what she said, but she talks about him so much I almost feel like I hate him, too."

Able wiped the sweat from his brow and his mind raced. He knew he had to get out of Rita's house and quick.

Kelli scraped eggs from the skillet onto her plate and asked, "Are you sure you don't want anything to eat?"

Able talked fast. "No thanks, Little Lady. As a matter of fact, I'd better get going," Able said, checking his watch. He stood and headed straight for the front door. Before he walked out, Able turned around and again tipped his imaginary hat and said, "It was real nice meeting you, Young Lady."

Kelli was half sorry to see Able leave and responded, "Yeah, you too, Able."

Then, like so many other Saturday mornings, after Rita had been drinking the Friday night before, Kelli sat down at the dining room table alone and ate breakfast. She was in the middle of devouring her large plate of bacon and eggs, when Rita crawled out of bed and asked where her boss, Mr. Taylor, had gone. Kelli knew right away she was toast.

Chapter 27
Rachel

It was Rachel's ninety-ninth attempt to lose weight. She had tried a grapefruit diet she found in Vogue magazine. The diet required she eat a piece of grapefruit after each small meal to burn the fat. Since she was accustomed to gorging on large meals, she ate a whole grapefruit after every meal. To Rachel's dismay she gained three pounds that week.

Once she set out to consume only a bag of grapes for the week. She had seen an anorexic girl do the same on an after-school special. Yet, Rachel only made it as far as the very first afternoon before she discarded the grapes in the trash can of the cafeteria. She readily ordered a generous helping of Sloppy Joes, tater tots, mixed vegetables and two cartons of chocolate milk. Her weight stayed the same that week.

Still, once and for all she remained determined more than ever to lose her unwanted pounds and shrink her ever increasing derriere. Just the week prior Mrs. Pettigrew had forbidden Rachel to wear her favorite khaki skirt, because it was too tight on Rachel's behind. Rachel begged her mother not to throw out the skirt, but to hang it in the back of the closet. Rachel convinced Mrs. Pettigrew she had been jogging and with the pounds melting away so quickly, Rachel would be able to fit into her beloved skirt again. Jogging only lasted two days.

She mustered her will power and hadn't eaten anything in two days. In all, she weighed herself six times on the bathroom scale during the fast. Finally, the needle budged, revealing a one pound weight loss. Still, when she turned around to look at her naked body in the full-length mirror, her *Bertha Butt* was still there. It refused to shrink and she refused to give up. She was determined to starve herself for an eternity if necessary to get her rear-end slim.

So, Rachel went down to the basement and turned up the record player and danced and jumped around just like she had witnessed Richard Simmons on General Hospital. She began to sweat and could feel the pounds melting away. It encouraged her to bounce around more and the sweat increased. Her heart beat a million times a minute, but she knew she was on the right track.

The James Brown record repeated twice and Rachel knew she needed a new groove to keep her exercise vibes going. Rachel put on Michael Jackson's *Beat It* album. It provided plenty of incentive to take her to the point of pure exhaustion.

Once Rachel turned off the record player, she dragged her worn body up two flights of stairs to the bathroom. She stripped down to her birthday suit and, holding her breath, she tipped onto the bathroom scale. Blinking twice, the numbers came into focus, revealing a two-pound weight loss. She had finally found what worked for her. Aerobics. *Thank God for Richard Simmons*, she thought.

Chapter 28
Bianca

After finding her mother and Mr. Goode's wedding license, Bianca became intrigued with finding more clues about her family's past. Particularly since her mother was so tight lipped about anything having to do with her life before she met Mr. Goode. As far as April was concerned, that was when her life began. Bianca wondered excessively what that meant for her. She had been born before April and Mr. Goode's union. Bianca wondered about April's marriage to her father, her birth, and how and why that marriage ended. April had thought enough to accept a black man's hand in marriage. Bianca wanted to know why April divorced her father.

Bianca scavenged through April's lock box several more times, but it yielded no additional information about her past. She ventured up to the creaky attic with a million cobwebs, imagining its two million spiders. The single light bulb hanging from the ceiling offered little light and cast such frightening shadows; Bianca nearly pissed herself at the sound of her own heavy breathing. Still, she found nothing in the attic aside from a few boxes of old clothes, some broken toys and a huge cracked mirror that April had been asking Mr. Goode to replace since they moved into the house.

Bianca even tried to talk about marriage casually one day to her mother.

"How old were you when you got married, Mom?"

April looked at her child and responded, "Nineteen. Why?"

"I was just wondering how old I might be when I get married."

"Well, don't be in any rush. Nineteen was very young to get married, even during my day," April cautioned.

"Did you always plan on only getting married once?" Rachel asked, pushing the envelope.

April raised an eyebrow and leaned across the kitchen table, "Look, Bianca, don't go starting no shit with Mr. Goode at home. He won't like your line of questioning and neither do I."

Bianca dropped the subject. It was when she decided to search the garage that she discovered something that would change her life forever. She had waited patiently to be alone in the garage. It was difficult in a home with six other people to be alone to do anything. So Bianca had to take every possible opportunity and sometimes she had to make up opportunities. This time she had come home early from school and faked cramps on the afternoon April went to the market.

As soon as April backed the car out of the driveway, Bianca dashed out of the back door and into the unattached garage. She entered the garage from the side door. It was never locked, because there was no key provided to them when they bought the house. Mr. Goode had never placed a new lock on it. Bianca passed the mounds of toys belonging to her brothers and sisters and made a bee line to the back of the garage, where several boxes were kept on top of a huge black trunk. She was hopeful there had to be some clue hidden back there. Bianca dug head first into the boxes. She pulled out more old clothes, a musty old blanket and some old car magazines. Nothing. She pulled and tugged at the lock on the trunk and even tried a long nail and hammer to break into it. Yet, after putting several deep scratches into the trunk, she gave up and instead began replacing the boxes on top of the trunk.

When the box containing the car magazines fell over, a small plastic bag fell out onto the dusty floor. Bianca picked up the bag and inspected it carefully. She was certain it was marijuana. She had seen some of the kids at school roll up joints in the bathroom and they had even offered her one, but she had refused. *Mr.Goode's been out here getting high*, she thought to herself. *As if he wasn't spending enough of their money getting drunk every Friday night.*

Bianca shoved the bag of marijuana in her pocket, but knew Mr. Goode would miss it. She picked up one of her sister's toy doll cups from the garage floor and poured out a small amount of the marijuana into the cup. She tucked the plastic bag into the stack of magazines and returned the stack to the box.

She returned to the house and retrieved a piece of notebook paper from her book bag. Just like she had witnessed the girls in the bathroom, Bianca cut a small piece of notebook paper and poured the marijuana inside. She licked the paper on one end and rolled the joint. It looked just like the others she had seen, except for the blue lines. Bianca took the treasure behind the garage, struck a match and greedily inhaled the smoke. She thought, *Mr. Goode has some nerve getting high, when I'm the one going through all the hell around here.* Although it was her first joint, it would not be her last.

Chapter 29

Curb Appeal

Rumors of Milo McFadden reached each of the three girls before they had the privilege of laying eyes on him. He would be a senior, like them, and was transferring from Forest Park to Fairfield. The rumor mill pegged Milo as the best athlete in the city in both football and basketball, hands down. If he lived up to his reputation, Fairfield High was certain to win state twice in one year.

As the captain of the cheerleading squad, Bianca heard from some of the football players that Milo would arrive just in time for summer football conditioning. His strength earned him the nickname *The Hulk* from his peers and competitors. Bianca imagined a huge mass of muscles, an angry face and green skin. She imagined this Milo McFadden to be repulsive and was in no rush to meet him.

Kelli was the next to hear about Milo from some of the boys on the varsity basketball team. They were all excited about the next best thing coming to their school. The team's superstar had graduated the previous spring and they desperately needed a strong man. Milo McFadden would fill the gap on the team. Kelli had been close to Greg, one of the basketball players, and was interested in becoming exclusive with him. Thus, Milo was not her concern; Greg was her love interest.

Rachel was the last to hear about Milo. She heard from her father that he would be getting a new church secretary, Mrs. McFadden, by the end of the summer. Mrs. McFadden's oldest son would be a senior and Rev. Pettigrew hoped she would befriend the young man at school and church. Ms. Elsie, who had been the secretary since Rev. Pettigrew's father was in the pulpit, would be retiring. Mrs. Pettigrew was knee-deep in organizing a retirement party for Ms. Elsie and she had drafted Rachel to assist her. Rachel was not looking forward to helping her mother or having some new boy tag along with her at school and church.

The girls had all compared notes about this Milo McFadden. They laughed at how each of them had heard about the newcomer, before his arrival. Rachel complained that she thought Milo was going to be a pain in her side and his mother was causing her additional work at home, because she was taking Ms. Elsie's job. So what the old woman could not type in order to prepare the weekly church bulletin or speak coherently to give the church announcements. She could still manage to answer the telephone, which was what she was hired to do.

Still, overall the girls had not given Milo, the new boy, much thought. That was until one summer evening at the neighborhood park, where the upperclassmen hung out. It was one of the hottest days of summer. As the three friends approached the park they noticed a group of boys playing basketball on the court and a large group of girls watching on the sidelines.

"The park is full," Kelli commented enthusiastically.

"It's our last weekend of freedom before school starts," Rachel commented snobbishly.

Suddenly there was a huge roar coming from the court and the sidelines as one of the boys jumped high into the air, and dunked the ball into the basket with great manly force. This was uncommon to see amongst the high school students, only seen when viewing a college game on TV.

"Wow!" Bianca exclaimed.

Kelli and Rachel were left with their mouths hanging open.

As they approached the group of blushing girls, Bianca asked, "Who's that?"

One of the familiar girls responded, "That's Milo McFadden!"

The girls each looked at one another and then back to the court at Milo as he shared high fives with some of the other guys on the court. They saw him as tall, dark and handsome—a strikingly gorgeous face atop a perfectly chiseled athlete's physique. They each licked their lips and silently wondered just how fast they could get closer to Milo McFadden.

Chapter 30
Kelli

Rita asked Kelli to attend an appointment with her immediately after school. She did not say where they were going or why. Kelli thought Rita had been acting strange lately. She wondered if Rita had fallen off the wagon again, or if it had something to do with her boss, Able Taylor. He had been calling for Rita almost every day and night. So despite wanting to hang out with Greg after school, Kelli walked straight home and waited for Rita.

When Rita arrived, the two hopped inside the car and Rita explained that she and Kelli were driving to West Chester to an alcohol treatment center. Kelli wanted to help her mother, but was reluctant to go.

"But why me? Shouldn't an adult go with you? What about Ms. Tracy?"

Rita took a deep breath before responding, "Kelli I know I'm asking a lot of you, but I really need you. Besides, I asked Tracy to go with me and she can't. She doesn't have anyone to watch the twins."

"What about her boyfriend?" Kelli protested.

"He moved out last week and her mother's in the same nursing home as Grammy. There's no one else. I need you, Kelli."

"Well, what about Able? He calls you every day. Why can't he go to alcohol treatment with you?"

"I talked to the counselor about Able. She didn't think it was a good idea, since we're only dating. I need to bring someone I have a long lasting relationship with." Rita reached over and pinched Kelli on her cheek, at the exact spot of her dimple. "I've known you for seventeen years, that's pretty long-lasting, don't you think?"

"You and Able are really dating? It wasn't long ago that all you could talk about was how much you hated him."

"You'll find out when you get older, but there's a thin line between love and hate." Rita blushed, embarrassed talking about her love life. It was the first time she'd had a love life to speak of since Jackson.

"So now we're both dating. You and Able and me and Greg," Kelli reflected.

"Yes, like two grown women," Rita said and smiled at Kelli.

Kelli had felt grown up for a long time now. She had to grow up with her mother in and out of a drunken state over the last few years. Now Rita wanted her to attend alcohol treatment. Kelli didn't know what to expect. Her first concern was that it was taking her away from spending time with Greg and her other friends. Besides, she wasn't sure how she could help Rita stop drinking. Lord knows she had tried. She had poured out Rita's beer time and time again, but it never stopped her mother from drinking.

When they arrived at the alcohol treatment center, which looked like nothing more than a doctor's office, the patients were separated from the family members. Kelli found herself the youngest in her group. There were spouses, parents and adult children, but no one still in high school like she.

Pat, a middle-aged female counselor, began to talk about the family member's role in the Intensive Outpatient Program. Kelli found herself focusing on the lines around Pat's eyes and those that formed around her mouth as she talked. Pat wore dumpy clothes and instead of listening to what she said, Kelli imagined Pat in a tight pair of *Guess* jeans and a *Ralph Lauren* button-down. She then imagined Pat with long straight hair instead of the frizzy blonde mass that sat on top of her head. She thought maybe if Pat were twenty years younger, they may be able to relate to one another. Perhaps Pat could understand her plight. Kelli didn't want to be there with Rita and felt like a hostage.

Still, Pat was able to gain Kelli's attention when she explained the purpose and rules of the family participant's first assignment. Each was to write how the patient's drinking had affected their lives. The counselor gave a few examples and Kelli's mind began to race.

She had taken care of Rita when she was passed out drunk, foregoing a mother who no longer took care of her. She had lied to teachers about why her mother couldn't attend teacher's conferences. She made up excuses to her coaches about why Rita couldn't attend her basketball, track and field awards ceremonies. She covered up for Rita when she didn't attend revival with the Pettigrews. She made up fabrications to her friends over and over again about illnesses that her mother had, to account for her shortcomings. She often prepared her own meals and ate them alone. Money for lunch, groceries or new clothing was inconsistent, because Rita often missed work. After Kelli looked at her list it made perfect sense that she was present for alcohol treatment with Rita. Her mother's drinking had affected her in ways she had never thought about before.

Still, it pained Kelli when she read her list in front of Rita and the entire group. When tears welled up in Kelli's eyes and she began to cry, Pat came over to her side and held her hand.

Chapter 31
Rachel

At her first opportunity, Rachel began sucking up to Mrs. McFadden, the new church secretary and Milo McFadden's mother. Right away she learned Mrs. McFadden's sister resided in Fairfield and had been recently widowed. The family's move allowed the McFaddens to offer her sister greater moral support as she raised her five young children alone. Rachel was empathetic as Mrs. McFadden shared her sister's misfortune.

Milo was their older son and Maurice, their younger son, was in junior high school. Maurice was a fierce athlete like his older brother. Mrs. McFadden said her boys were as close as two brothers could be, although they were four years apart in age. Milo was a good student, but found English to be his weakest subject. Rachel chimed right in and offered to tutor Milo in English as she received all A's and B's in her course work.

As her father suggested, Rachel walked to school with Milo the first week of school and showed him around. Rachel was elated as she walked into the school with the most popular boy —handsome and a star athlete. Milo joined Rachel at her exclusive lunch table and all the other girls were green with envy. The guys flocked around Milo as they wished to be connected with his greatness. Milo and Rachel began what she hoped to be a lasting friendship that would quickly blossom into a hot and steamy romance.

Typically after dinner each Monday Rachel tutored Milo at the Pettigrew's dining room table. Of course, Rev. and Mrs. Pettigrew overlooked their sessions from a close distance. The sessions were to allow Rachel to guide Milo through the week's English assignments, but Rachel had ulterior motives. Rachel imagined each week that it would be the day that Milo made his move. Each Monday she dressed especially for him and styled her hair with extra care. She brushed her teeth thoughtfully and smiled into the mirror, happy she had gone through the torture of braces to make her smile perfect and inviting for Milo. She lightly applied make up to give herself the appearance that she naturally had a smooth complexion and rosy cheeks. Once their hands accidentally touched flipping the page of Milo's English book and Rachel was certain he felt the same electricity pulse through his veins that she had. They would be the perfect couple as soon as he opened his eyes to what he had right in front of him.

"Your composition outline seems to be coming along just fine," Rachel commented as she held onto Milo's notebook. Just holding onto the book that he touched only moments ago was a thrill that made Rachel feel warm and fuzzy inside.

"Yeah, it's coming along, but it's torture every step of the way. I hate this stuff," Milo commented with a half-smile.

"It's really not that bad," Rachel blushed.

"Not for you. This comes easy for you, but I don't really care about it one way or another. Especially not right now. Our big game against Princeton High is coming up this Friday. I have three new plays to learn. I don't know where I'm going to find the time to get this all done," Milo said exasperated. He leaned back in his chair and rubbed his face over and over again with his hands.

Rachel wanted to do whatever she could. Of course, in her mind, the two were only days away from being a couple and since he was going to be her boyfriend, she thought, *why not?*

Rachel put her hand on Milo's knee, looked deep into his eyes and whispered, "Don't worry about this outline. I'll finish it for you."

Milo smiled and whispered in return, "Would you do that for me, Rachel?"

The way he whispered her name made Rachel's knees weak. She was glad she was sitting or she may have lost her footing at that very moment.

"Sure. It's no problem, Milo. Really," she said, blushing profusely.

"My mom said you were the greatest and she was right."

Rachel was glad he and his mother had been talking about her at home.

Milo stood up from the table and said loud enough for Rev. and Mrs. Pettigrew to hear him in the next room, "Well, I guess I'll see you at school tomorrow."

Rev. Pettigrew responded, "Are you young people done already?"

"Yes, we're all done, Rev. Pettigrew," Rachel responded, rolling her eyes.

She and Milo shared a private laugh as Rachel walked Milo to the door. He walked out, leaving Rachel disappointed at not receiving the hug she had been hoping to get all day.

* * * *

At Milo's locker the next day, Rachel handed him the notebook with the completed composition outline inside.

"Thanks a million, Rachel, you don't know how much this helps me," Milo said, putting the notebook away in his locker.

"I don't mind," Rachel confessed. She took a step closer, entering into Milo's personal space and clearly within kissing distance. "I don't mind at all. In fact, if there's anything else I can do to help you, just let me know, Milo."

He leaned in, their lips nearly touching. "Do you really mean that?" he asked with a smile.

"Sure. Just ask me anything," she begged.

"Well, there is something else I wanted to ask you, but I don't know if I should," he cautioned.

"Go ahead," she insisted.

"I don't know. My mom said I shouldn't."

Rachel panicked. She thought her attempts at getting close to Mrs. McFadden had backfired. Now, his mother was telling him to treat her like a young lady, when all she wanted was for Milo to kiss her and set her body on fire.

"Come on now, don't be a mama's boy," she prodded him. "Go ahead and ask me."

She kept her face as close to his as possible.

"Okay," he said, looking deep into Rachel's eyes. "Can you hook me up with your fine friend, Bianca?" he asked seriously.

Rachel stopped breathing and her heart sank into her stomach. "Bianca?"

"Yeah, she's the finest thing I've ever seen!" Milo boasted, grinning ear to ear.

Rachel's blood began to boil and she found herself saying, "Bianca's a ho! You don't wanna mess with her!" She stormed away, leaving Milo standing alone. By the time she found herself midway down the hall, she had half a mind to go back and tear up that composition outline she had worked all night to perfect.

Chapter 32
Bianca

Milo worked his connections and found a way to be introduced to Bianca. Soon the two were talking on the telephone every night for hours. John Jr. complained to Mr. Goode that Bianca was hogging the phone and Mommy started asking questions about who she was talking to. April Goode's stares were accusatory each time Bianca answered the phone. April had warned Bianca to stay away from boys. Bianca lied to her mother that Milo was just a friend from school. Soon, she started making calls to Milo from Kelli's house next door.

Bianca and Milo's infatuation with one another grew with every call. In mere weeks Milo was carrying Bianca's books home from school, careful to part at the corner at the end of her street. Bianca had to be mindful not to let Mommy or

Mr. Goode know she was spending any time at all with Milo, because she knew they would not approve. In fact, she was certain she would be punished severely.

Soon they were an official couple and began holding hands through the hallway of the school. Each day long notes to one another were shared about their thoughts and feelings. They didn't make a move without including the other. They ate lunch together, although some of her friends protested about having Milo and his buddies overcrowd their table. Bianca and Milo dressed alike with the clothes she stole for herself. They seldom went out alone. They were no longer individuals, but a package deal.

In the fall, as captain of the cheerleading squad, Bianca cheered Milo on at every football game and in the winter she was his number one fan at each basketball game. Everyone noticed and thought they were the most attractive and popular couple in school. Everyone that is, except Rachel. While Rachel moved on, she didn't forget for a long time how Milo chose Bianca over her and she held a fierce grudge. The jealously put a huge wedge between any hopes of her maintaining a healthy relationship with Bianca.

Moreover, as with most young adults, Milo's and Bianca's relationship began to move forward. Soon hugging and French kissing was not enough for either of them. On New Year's Eve, when Bianca said she was spending the night with Kelli, she met Milo at the corner at the end of her street and ventured away with him for the night.

She jumped into the passenger's side of Milo's father's car. "Wow, it's freezing outside," she said, bringing the collar of her coat close around her face and brushing off a light sprinkle of snow.

Milo cranked up the heat, "You should've let me pick you up at Kelli's house."

"No way! If Mommy or Mr. Goode would've seen you, I would be on punishment until graduation!" Bianca shared lightly, but the sentiment was serious.

"They're going to have to accept us sooner or later. Bianca, you're almost eighteen. Almost a full grown woman and we're sneaking around like a couple of kids."

"I told you, Mommy will never approve of me dating."

"Anyone?" Milo paused, "Or any black man?"

"Anyone," Bianca replied. "There's no point in my even trying to talk to her about it." She reached over and kissed Milo softly on the cheek as they sped off down the street with Sade's single, *The Sweetest Taboo,* crooning loudly on the radio. Just the two of them, alone.

Bianca reached over and held Milo's hand. "Where are we going tonight, the movies?"

Milo shook his head no.

"Out to eat?"

Again Milo shook his head no.

"Then where?"

"To my house. To be alone," he said, with a hint of nervousness in his voice. He looked over at Bianca. "No one's home. They'll be out for a while."

"Everybody?" she asked.

He nodded, "Everybody."

A few silent minutes passed between them. "Are you okay with us being alone?" he asked carefully.

They had talked about spending some time alone. They would sneak five minutes alone after school in the stairwell or ten minutes at Kelli's house when Rita was gone. Aside from a movie theatre sitting in their own row or a restaurant sitting alone in a booth, the two had never spent any significant amount of time alone. Milo talked about it more and more and he even asked Bianca if she was ready to take their relationship to the next level. She was ready, but had no idea tonight was going to be the night until Milo had just announced it.

Bianca looked at Milo adoringly. "I'm fine with it," she answered with a smile.

"Cool," he said and within minutes he maneuvered the car to his driveway.

When they arrived at the McFadden house everyone was gone indeed. They walked slowly up the stairs to Milo's bedroom and chatted nervously while sitting on his bed. Milo turned the radio on softly and they listened to the 1985 top 100 hit songs being counted down. Although familiar with one another, their kisses seemed awkward. Still it wasn't long before they undressed, lay in Milo's bed and made love together for the first time. It felt right to Bianca. She didn't feel violated or betrayed, like she had with Mr. Goode or Dion. Thankfully, for the first time in her life, with Milo, Bianca felt loved.

Chapter 33
Support Beams

Rachel drove cautiously in Mrs. Pettigrew's car the entire seven miles to Elder-Berman's Department Store with Kelli riding shot gun and Bianca sitting in the back seat. She nearly took out two mailboxes and an old lady with a shopping cart, attempting to cross over Main Street at a major intersection. Kelli screamed out all three times and Rachel said the screams were unjustified and were making her nervous. Still, somehow the girls and the car arrived at their destination for the shopping trip without a scratch.

Kelli jumped out of the car as soon as Rachel parked in the lot sideways, taking up three separate parking spaces. She checked her purse to make sure she had enough bus fare in case she was not feeling brave enough to take the car ride back with Rachel.

Bianca opened the back car door and immediately vomited her lunch on the ground. Rachel accused Bianca of vomiting inside Mrs. Pettigrew's car and the two began to bicker right away. Like clockwork, Kelli stood between the two of them.

"Do I need to remind you ladies, we're here to shop, not fight. Come on, you guys. We're supposed to be hanging out and having a good time."

"If Bianca is sick she should've stayed home. That's all I'm saying. Mrs. Pettigrew will kill me if there's vomit in her car," Rachel raged.

"Okay. Okay," Kelli said. "Bianca already said she didn't vomit in the car. She opened the door and stuck her head out. Now come on. Let's find a rest room inside. It's cold out here."

Rachel locked the car and the three went inside Elder-Berman's in search of the restroom. Bianca headed straight for the sink and stuck her hands out, filling them with water and bringing her hands up to her lips. She swished the water in her mouth and spit it back out into the sink. Kelli handed Bianca a hand full of paper towels as Rachel primped in the mirror several feet away.

"Are we ready to shop now?" Kelli asked of her two friends.

Rachel and Bianca smiled at Kelli, without looking at one another and answered in unison, "Ready."

Kelli had as much money as Rita had been able to give her for clothing in a very long time. Rita had been consistent with alcohol treatment and had been attending work on a regular basis. In turn, Rita's paychecks had been consistent and once again there was extra money for clothing. Kelli was grateful; it was nice to be out with her friends, even if the two of them were not getting along that day.

Rachel had Rev. and Mrs. Pettigrew's charge card in her wallet, along with a note from Mrs. Pettigrew giving her permission to use the card. Besides, most of the salespeople knew Mrs. Pettigrew and Rachel personally in every department store in the small town. They frequented the store so often that Rachel knew the store and the merchandise like the back of her hand.

Bianca had to be careful in the store. She had stolen there several times before. She had returned some stolen items from other stores and had some cash on hand from the bogus returns. Still, she knew it was almost impossible for her to resist stealing something she desperately wanted from any store. It was as if she were compelled to steal with no personal will power.

It was the formal dresses in the juniors department that captured the attention of all three girls, sparking excitement about the senior prom. This would be the prom to end all proms. They reveled in the excitement and decided their prom dresses would be their next shopping trip and it would be an out-of-town trip. They couldn't dare walk inside the prom wearing local dresses.

* * * *

A stop at McDonald's on the way home finished their trip. Rachel was the first at the counter with her ravenous appetite, ready to order a Big Mac and the infamous French fries. Kelli followed right behind her. The smell of the greasy food sent Bianca running to the restroom. Kelli found Bianca bent over the toilet. For the second time that day, Kelli handed Bianca a hand full of paper towels to clean up.

Bianca looked at herself in the mirror and then back at Kelli. "It's Rachel's driving. All of that zigging and zagging and breaking so hard, has my nerves on edge."

Kelli looked at Bianca and raised both eyebrows. "So it's Rachel's driving, huh?"

"Yeah. That's it," Bianca said meekly.

One of the restaurant workers entered the restroom and entered a stall. The girls just stared at one another until the worker came out, washed her hands and exited the restroom.

"Is that why you didn't try any clothes on at the mall?" Kelli accused.

"What are you talking about, Kelli?"

"I'm talking about the fact that I know you, Bianca. I know something is wrong."

"Nothing's wrong with me, I swear."

That's when Kelli pulled out the trump card.

"Bianca *Truth or Dare*?"

Tears began to well inside Bianca's eyes and she knew she could no longer dance around the truth.

"*Truth,*" she squealed through the tears.

"What's your secret?"

Bianca melted into Kelli's arms and confessed, "I'm pregnant." Her revelation came just as Rachel walked inside the room.

Chapter 34
Kelli

The girls took a vote and decided Rita was the best adult to approach regarding Bianca's predicament. She was the least likely to tell April and Mr. Goode. She was the least likely to judge and most likely to help. So the three girls found themselves huddled in Rita's living room confessing to Rita about Bianca's unplanned and unwanted pregnancy. Kelli sat on one side of Bianca and Rachel sat on the other.

"Bianca, you have to tell the young man you're pregnant," Rita shared.

Through her panic and confusion that she had been holding inside for several days Bianca insisted, "I can't. He'll hate me. He'll think I'm trying to trap him!" She gasped for breath. "I mean I love him, but I don't want a baby now. Besides, a baby will ruin everything. We're planning on going to college!"

Rachel looked at Bianca and despite the seriousness of the situation; all she managed to do was pick apart Bianca's statement. She was certain Bianca had not applied to a single college, so she wondered who this *we* was that was planning on going to college.

"Besides, my mother and Mr. Goode will kill me. They'll kick me straight out of the house. My mother has so much as told me herself!"

"Calm down now," Rita directed her. "First things first. You have to tell the young man and I insist on that. Any decision about your pregnancy is not your decision alone."

Kelli spoke up and asked, "Should she call him now?"

Rachel blurted out, "You don't break that kind of news over the telephone. She has to tell him in person."

"I think that would be best," Rita agreed. "You two are going to have to talk about this."

Bianca's eyes flooded with tears, "No, this is all my fault. I have to take care of this myself."

"Wait a minute," Rita spoke up and almost lost her temper. As an unwed teen mother herself, Rita's blood boiled quickly as Bianca took on all the responsibility for her unplanned pregnancy. In Rita's situation, Jackson had been older and married, but still he was just as responsible for bringing their child into the world as she. And even after putting up with twelve years of his lies to leave his marriage, he had walked out on her and Kelli. Jackson was the one averting responsibility, not Rita. Still, Rita took a deep breath before responding to Bianca, who was only a child and did not have the benefit of Rita's vast years of experience. She spoke calmly when she said, "It takes two to make a baby. You didn't have sex by yourself. You didn't get pregnant by yourself. This is not your decision alone. There has to be a conversation."

"We don't have to tell his parents, do we?" Bianca asked. "I don't want them to be mad at Milo."

"Why don't you and Milo talk first and the two of you can decide who needs to get involved after that."

Bianca stood and hugged Rita, Kelli and Rachel. She thanked them all for their help and for listening to her. She then wiped her face quickly and ran home before curfew. The last thing she needed now was to be grounded.

Before Kelli and Rachel could escape from Rita's grasp she scolded, "And the two of you sit back down!"

Kelli and Rachel were confused, because they didn't think they had done anything wrong. In fact, they had brought Bianca to Rita. The one adult they felt they could trust. Still, they hurriedly planted their behinds on the sofa across from Rita.

Rita narrowed her eyes at the two. "Birds of a feather flock together!" she announced boldly. "Now, have the two of you been sexually active?"

Rachel was the first to speak, "I don't believe in sex before marriage."

"Don't give me that holier-than-thou line of bull," Rita commanded. "Your grandfather was a minister and all three of your aunties were pregnant before they graduated from high school."

Rachel knew this to be true. Sometimes she forgot what a small town Fairfield was. "Honestly, Ms. Rita, I'm not having sex." Rachel held up her right hand, "I swear."

"And you?" Rita asked of Kelli.

"I'm not having sex," Kelli said. "Honestly."

"Let me tell the two of you something. Yes, I was pregnant with Kelli at seventeen. Pregnancy with teenage girls is contagious. One gets pregnant and before you know it, half of the school is pregnant. Before I could give birth to Kelli, my two best friends were pregnant, which is why I'm looking at the two of you."

Kelli and Rachel, as though on cue, looked at one another and then back at Rita.

"Speak up now. *Planned Parenthood* gives free birth control pills and condoms," Rita stated flatly.

Chapter 35
Rachel

Rachel thought about Bianca's pregnancy nearly night and day. Although Milo had foolishly stepped over her to get to Bianca, still somehow her heart went out to Bianca. Seventeen years old and pregnant was not how Rachel wanted to go out. She had an image to uphold. Not just because she was the daughter of Rev. Pettigrew, but because she had her own dreams and plans for her life. Her dreams included going to college, pledging a sorority and starting a career, before she started her family. She also thought about what Rita said and she thought about Planned Parenthood. She knew where it was, all of the teenagers did, because like Rita said, they gave out free birth control pills and condoms. Rachel wasn't having sex yet. Sure she had come close. She had given a boy a hand job, so she knew the inevitable was near. To protect her image, Rachel skipped morning classes one day and paid a visit to Planned Parenthood.

Chapter 36

Bianca

Milo agreed. The best thing to do was for Bianca to get an abortion. It would take most of the money he had saved from working over the summer, but it would make sure he and Bianca were not faced with a responsibility they were not prepared to handle. That's what he had explained to her.

He borrowed his mother's car and drove Bianca to the Women's Clinic, a forty-minute drive. They didn't speak a word during the ride. They walked in together and Bianca checked in at the nurse's station. She lied about her age, because without parental permission she could not get an abortion at the clinic at seventeen. She was only a few months shy of legal. They sat in silence for nearly an hour as they waited. Bianca wondered silently if this was her opportunity to think and change her mind. But, there was no way. She couldn't. Their minds were made up. Milo had been offered athletic scholarships at all three of the schools he wanted to attend. He simply had to select one. He would play football at the college level, earn his degree and become a professional player. Their lives would be set. There would be plenty of time for a baby later.

Bianca would wait for Milo while he attended college. Although her grades were not up to par to attend a four-year college, she considered beauty school or a two-year business college. She could work and attend school part time. She and Kelli were thinking about getting an apartment together. Kelli was sure she could get a job where Rita worked, since Able Taylor was a big shot there. Their plans were coming together and there was no room for a baby.

Finally Bianca's name was called. She was led into a bathroom to take a urine pregnancy test and asked to remove all of her clothing except her bra and socks. She dressed in the hospital gown left hanging on the hook on the back of the door. With the jar of urine left on the back of the toilet and her hands full with her clothing and shoes, she departed the bathroom. An attendant rushed in and retrieved the urine sample and led her to another waiting area. There were four other women there, all waiting in hospital gowns and holding their clothes and shoes in their hands, just the same as she. One of the girls looked just as young as she, but she was popping gum and bopping her head to a Walkman. The same attendant returned with a tray and passed out a single pill and a Dixie cup of water to each of the women. The pill would make them *relax.* The young girl with the Walkman never stopped bopping, nor did she unplug the headphones to hear the information about the pill, but she popped it into her mouth and downed it with the small cup of water. No one looked the others in the eyes. Bianca sat staring at the pink socks on her feet. Finally the attendant returned and called "Terri", but no one moved. Finally the woman sitting next to the Walkman girl tapped her shoulder and Terri rose from her seat, gathered her belongings and was escorted down the hallway for surgery.

One by one, the other three ladies left the small waiting room, until Bianca was the last person remaining. Bianca waited alone until her guilt and shame rose fully in her throat and began to choke her. The moment before she was sure she was going to lose consciousness, the attendant returned and called her name. On her walk down the hallway she could hear each breath she took as they vibrated from her chest cavity and resounded loudly in her ears.

Chapter 37
Open House

High School graduation far outweighed all other life accomplishments for Kelli, Rachel and Bianca. There had been many mountains and valleys in their early relationship, but now their lives together and apart would mature and compound. They were each at the cusp of making decisions that would affect the rest of their lives forever.

It was just minutes before Rachel's open house began and the girls were together for the final time in Rachel's childhood bedroom. Sure, their futures would bring them together again, but it would be their last time together in that place. Rachel's bedroom was the white and pink sanctuary where together they had shared secrets, gossip and precious dreams. Under Reverend Pettigrew's roof and, at times, with Mrs. Pettigrew's ear pressed firmly against the door.

Rachel sat upright in her desk chair, while Kelli curled Rachel's hair with an electric curling iron. Bianca lay casually across Rachel's canopy bed.

"My party starts in thirty minutes, so I'm going to need you to do the best you can, because I have to be on time to greet my guests. Mrs. Pettigrew insists that I, personally, escort everyone to the back yard picnic," Rachel hurriedly said, pressed for time.

Kelli picked up the curling iron and looked at it seriously. "This is a curling iron, not a magic wand. You should've rolled your hair last night, instead of blow drying it. Your hair is a thick, frizzy mess," she said harshly to Rachel, and busied herself trying to straighten and curl the hair all at once.

"I know, but I came home late last night from my date with Darren Jenkins," Rachel explained, hoping her friends would want to know more.

"Darren! You're seeing Darren again?" Bianca asked.

"Yeah. We're not exclusive, but I went out to the movies with him last night." Then she whispered, "Afterwards we went back to his apartment." She was always mindful of Mrs. Pettigrew's listening ear.

"His apartment?" Bianca whispered and sat up on the edge of the bed to hear more.

"Yes, his apartment," Rachel explained, still keeping her voice low. "He's renting an apartment from his cousin for the summer vacation until he goes back to Tennessee State this fall. He has an internship with an insurance company, so he's making big bucks. It's so nice being with a college boy, they really know how to treat you. He brought me flowers, paid for the movie and popcorn. Then he took me back to his place for a glass of wine."

"And what did he expect in return?" Kelli, the mother figure in the group, asked accusingly.

"Nothing. I mean we kissed and messed around a little, but he didn't expect anything and I didn't give up anything." Rachel paused and then commented, "Not yet anyway, but the summer is still young," she smiled.

Bianca fell back onto the bed and laughed herself silly, while Kelli shook her head and pursed her lips. Once Bianca gained her composure, she cautioned Rachel, "Be careful, Rach. When you're ready, make sure you use protection." Bianca's mind flashed back to her trip to the Women's Clinic. Her mind returned there each time someone talked about sex and whenever she and Milo made love. She was on birth control pills, but still the threat of pregnancy remained forever present.

"Don't worry," Rachel said, "Darren has that covered. He said he has a nightstand drawer full of condoms with my name on them!"

"And how did condoms come up in the conversation?" Kelli asked.

"That was when he offered her something to drink at his place," Bianca suggested. "Coffee, tea, condoms?"

Kelli laughed and accidentally burned the back of Rachel's neck with the curling iron.

Rachel yelled out in pain.

"Don't blame me. It's Bianca's fault. Tell her to stop cracking jokes. She should be the one over here curling your hair anyway. She's the one going to beauty school."

"Anyway, did you hear back from them?" Rachel asked Bianca.

"Yes, I start in September. Now I just have to come up with the money. I need to get a job this summer, I guess. But I wanted to spend my summer with Milo before he leaves for Ohio State. He won't be able to get home often between football and his studies."

"What about you, Rachel, did you hear from any of the colleges you applied to?" Kelli asked.

"Only one," Rachel answered. She had not told her friends she had only applied to one college. It was the same college where a certain boy she had had her eye on during her entire senior year was attending. The one boy she nearly had in her grasp and continued to dream about each night. The only one she could see herself giving her virginity to. The only boy she thought she would ever love. "I'm going to Ohio State," She announced. She turned to Bianca and offered, "I'll keep an eye on Milo for you."

Bianca knew Rachel's offer was not an innocent one. She was sure Rachel was after her man, but she felt confident in her relationship with Milo. They were in love and their love was destined to last forever. Milo had told her so himself.

"What about you, Kelli?" Rachel wanted to know, "Did you make it into the Kelly School of Business?"

"Yes. I got my letter from them last week, but I'm not sure if I'm going to attend now."

"Why not?" Rachel asked.

Kelli nonchalantly responded. She had been keeping a fantastic secret from her friends since senior prom night. "Did I tell you guys Greg asked me to marry him?"

Chapter 38
Kelli

The wedding would have a Christmas theme, Rita decided. Together, Rita and Kelli shopped excessively for her gown, bridesmaids's dresses, invitations and a wedding cake. Kelli could not believe her mother was so excited about her marriage to Greg. It was almost as if Rita was getting married instead of Kelli. Rita had gone over the guest list a dozen times and it was clear, Rita invited more of her friends than Kelli's. Still it was good for the two of them to have something to do together.

Rita's joy was the exact opposite of the disdain Greg's mother, Patty, felt about the pending nuptials. Patty, a widow since Greg was a baby, refused to accept her son was an adult or that he could make such a decision about marriage. Patty thought Greg was too young to get married, although she had been married to Greg's father at seventeen. Also, Greg's decision to marry a girl who had been born out of wedlock was scandalous according to Patty. She thought the whole matter was shameful and Greg could find a much better girl than Kelli Brown. At one point, Patty even refused to attend the ceremony.

For Kelli the expense of putting together a formal wedding complete with all of the trimmings soon mounted. Kelli was working an entry-level job in Rita's office, thanks to Able Taylor. Greg was working a factory job. Both were making little more than minimum wage. At the same time, they were saving to move into a small apartment after the wedding and would need furniture and other household items. Before they were even married, their finances were strained. Kelli felt the strain with each purchase, but Greg seemed oblivious. He contributed less to the wedding expenses than he promised and soon Kelli found herself cutting corners and scaling down the wedding plans.

In the midst of the wedding preparations and drama with Greg's mother, Grammy's health went from bad to devastating. She had been placed in hospice following yet another stroke and Rita was prompted to settle Grammy's affairs before the end of the summer. Grammy had fought the good fight for nearly an entire decade in that nursing home wilting away. Sadly, in the early summer,

Grammy gave up the ghost and was laid to rest for the final time. Long-lost relatives appeared out of the woodwork for Grammy's funeral service and Rita invited each one of them to Kelli's wedding, much to Kelli's chagrin.

* * * *

All in one summer, Kelli was planning a wedding, buried her grandmother and her best friend was leaving to go away to college. She and Rachel had barely spent any time together that summer. Following high school graduation, Kelli immediately started working full time and Rachel had busied herself with college preparations and chasing Darren Jenkins all summer.

The weekend before Rachel left to attend freshman orientation at Ohio State, Kelli helped Rachel pack for college. Rachel pulled stacks of clothes from her closet and Kelli folded them neatly and tried her best to squeeze them inside three pink suitcases.

"So your summer fling is over with Darren?" Kelli asked.

"Yes. It was nice while it lasted and Darren is a really nice guy. He's just not the guy for me," Rachel said half-sad. "He's already back at Tennessee State. He left early this week. He called me this morning and wished me good luck and said he wanted to stay in touch. He even said I could call him collect from O State."

"That's pretty generous of him. It sounds like he doesn't want it to end."

"He started sniffing around me real hard, after we finally did it," Rachel said and smirked.

"So you finally went all the way," Kelli said jokingly. "You've been teasing that boy since he was in the eighth grade. What made you change your mind about waiting?"

Rachel stopped flinging clothes onto the bed momentarily and stared into space. "It's just that Darren is so doggone nice. He did everything I asked him to do, plus a whole bunch of stuff I didn't even ask for. I mean he did beg me for it all summer and I just felt like I owed it to him."

"Rachel, that's no reason to give up your virginity. You didn't owe Darren anything. You should've waited for love."

"Don't get me wrong," Rachel said, returning to emptying out her closet. "I love Darren, just not the same way I love Milo."

Kelli sighed heavily. "Rachel, you have to stop talking about Milo that way. Bianca and Milo are still together. They're in love. And besides, Bianca is our friend."

"Wrong." Rachel said harshly. Her evil side reared its ugly head. "Bianca is your friend. She and I aren't friends anymore. Not since she did what she did."

"What did Bianca ever do to you?"

"She stole Milo right from under my nose!"

"You and Milo were never a couple. The two of you had just met and were barely even friends."

Rachel stopped retrieving clothes again and placed her hands on her ample hips, "That's not true. I was nearly Milo's girlfriend, when Bianca sunk her claws into him and stole him right from under me. It's only because she was willing to give it up so fast, that he went after her. I just wasn't ready for all of that back then. Now that I'm ready, I'll get him back!"

Kelli stopped folding clothes and spoke softly, "Rachel, you have to stop. Whatever you thought was happening between you and Milo never came to be. Now Milo and Bianca are together. They were together almost all of their senior year. Now they're making plans together. She's going to wait for him to get out of college and they're going to get married."

Rachel returned her attention to packing and said defiantly, "Bianca's not going to O State with Milo. I am."

* * * *

The weekend before her wedding, Kelli had a proper bridal shower at Ms. Tracy's house. Mrs. Pettigrew and April Goode, who had grown fond of Kelli over the years, attended. She was showered with kitchen and bathroom items and made to feel like the beautiful blushing bride she would be the following week. However, her bachelorette party consisted of her and Bianca getting drunk in Bianca's tiny one-room apartment. Bianca moved into an efficiency apartment after finding a job at a grocery store, while she saved money for cosmetology school.

Kelli, a novice drinker, was drunk after only a few sips of wine. Still, it gave her the courage to do what she had been longing to do for years. Together, she and Bianca drove Greg's car to the corner grocery store and bought two dozen eggs. Then they drove to 1524 Grant Circle. She sat in front of the address and stared at Jackson Carter's old rusty brown car sitting in the driveway.

In her drunken haze, she talked herself into a rage. It wasn't difficult, with feelings of rage about their missing fathers brewing inside both girls' heads. Finally they got out of the car and egged Jackson's house. Kelli felt a sense of redemption and it lasted even after she sobered.

The next day was Kelli's and Greg's wedding day. Rita was there with bells on and Greg's mother's attitude was appropriately cordial for the occasion. Able Taylor offered to walk Kelli down the aisle. Until he offered, Kelli had no idea who would do the honor. There was no other man in her life, besides Rev. Pettigrew and he was officiating the service.

Kelli's bridesmaids, including Rachel, Bianca and three of her high school basketball team mates, descended upon her and helped to prepare her for the ceremony. It was a bit awkward with Rachel and Bianca barely speaking a word to one another, but still the preparations went off without a hitch. When she was ready, her bridesmaids preceded her down the center aisle of the church. Kelli took Able's arm and together they marched down the aisle to Greg who was waiting in front with Rev. Pettigrew. When asked, both Kelli and Greg responded, "I do."

When it was time for Mr. and Mrs. Greg Campbell to leave the church for the reception hall, Kelli thought she saw an old brown car sitting across the street from the church out of the corner of her eye. Kelli no longer cared about Jackson Carter. He had not cared about her when he walked out of her life. Kelli had a new man in her life, her husband.

Chapter 39
Rachel

College was horrible for Rachel's body image. So many of the other girls were paper thin and she thought it made her look like an Amazon in comparison. She found her way to the gym and worked out twice a week and took an aerobics class. Still, she struggled. The heavy cafeteria food put the weight right back on her hips, butt and thighs. Not to mention the late night pizza deliveries and care packages with homemade chocolate chip cookies from Mrs. Pettigrew.

Rachel thought the birth control pills she was taking may have been a part of her weight problem. She heard some of the other girls complaining about the pill making their skin break out and gain weight. Yet, the nurse at the student health center cautioned Rachel to continue to take the oral contraceptives. She told Rachel that fifty percent of girls who drop out of college, do so because they're pregnant and condoms alone are much less effective than birth control pills. With that information, Rachel kept the pills.

Yet, her solution to weight loss was just around the corner. One evening her roommate, a white girl named Lynn Dupree from Columbus, handed her a small white round pill, while they pulled an all-night study session for mid-term finals. Rachel stared at the small pill Lynn dropped on her desk.

"Come on, Rachel, don't, like, pull that preacher's daughter crap with me. I know you know what a *bennie* is."

"Honestly I don't, Lynn."

"Like, come on, Rachel. It's a *black beauty*."

Rachel still just stared at Lynn as if she were speaking French. Most of the time, with Lynn's valley-girl act Rachel hardly knew what Lynn was talking about half the time.

"Like it's totally *speed*."

"Yeah, I've heard of *speed*," Rachel confessed. "I saw a Phil Donahue episode where a bunch of housewives were on *speed* to keep up with their kids, husbands and house work and stuff."

"Yeah, *speed* will, like, help you do anything you wanna do." Lynn laid a few more of her private stash of *bennies* on Rachel's desk.

Rachel took one of the small pills and stashed the rest away in the bottom drawer of her desk. One of the other things Rachel remembered most about those women on the Phil Donahue show was that they were all thin as rails. If these *bennies*, *black beauties* or whatever they were called could help her to get thin, that's all Rachel really cared about.

* * * *

Quickly Rachel lost a significant amount of weight. Everyone commented on her lean physique. So Rachel paid Lynn for more pills, but soon, Lynn's stash was nearly depleted. Rachel was prepared to do anything to keep the flow of pills coming. She begged Lynn to get more of the *black beauties.* Lynn told Rachel it would cost her, the pills were not cheap. Rachel made a call to Mrs. Pettigrew and lied to her mother for the very first time in her life to get Mrs. Pettigrew to deposit money into her savings account.

So, on a Friday after midnight, Lynn and Rachel drove outside of Columbus to a motorcycle bar. Rachel had never seen anything like it before, other than television. The two walked inside and all eyes were immediately on them. Of course all the other patrons were dressed in black leather jackets. Apparently there was also a ten-tattoo minimum, because they had at least that many on their arms, necks and faces. At least the color of Lynn's skin was the same as everyone else's. Rachel nearly started to turn around and run out. Lynn sensed her hesitation and grabbed Rachel's arm and pulled her forward. Lynn walked straight to the back of the bar into the men's restroom. Of course inside there was a guy peeing at a urinal. The guy turned around and looked at them, but didn't seem to flinch. He zipped up his pants, didn't flush or wash his hands and walked out. Lynn and Rachel stood in place.

Rachel finally asked, "What are we waiting in here for?"

"For Zeus."

"Who is Zeus?"

"The guy with the *bennies*."

Rachel was scared. Here she stood, the only black person in a motorcycle bar an hour from campus, standing alone with a white girl from Columbus, who thought she was a valley girl. She began to think she had truly lost her mind, all in an effort to lose weight. Yet her mind flashed to Milo McFadden, his handsome face and his body, with firm and well-defined muscles and she waited patiently for Zeus.

Within minutes, the smallest biker in the bunch sashayed inside the men's room. He stood about four feet and ten inches tall. His hair, what was left of it along the sides and back, was long, greasy and disgusting. He had less than a dozen rotten teeth left in his mouth and when he spoke a foul order fought through the stench of urine and assaulted Rachel's olfactory senses.

Zeus looked at Lynn and asked, "How much?"

"Like 400," Lynn answered coolly.

Zeus turned his attention to Rachel. He looked her up and down and asked, "Is she part of my payment?"

"No, we, like, have cash," Lynn answered.

Zeus stood and stared at Rachel. He licked his lips and stated firmly, "I'm gonna need to see a little peek, when I come back." Then Zeus walked out.

Lynn turned to Rachel and suddenly her valley-girl speech was gone, "Look, Rachel, when he comes back we're gonna have to show him our tits."

"What? Are you kidding me!" Rachel yelled.

"Look, this isn't your pediatrician's office in case you didn't notice! Zeus is a sick puppy, but trust me, there are worse out there. Either show him your tits and give him the money or he won't give you the pills. Now do you want them or not?"

Rachel wanted the pills.

* * * *

The next time Rachel ran into Milo at the student center, she ran up to him and hugged him. As he wrapped his arms around her, even he commented that she was looking svelte. It made Rachel feel good that Milo's hands lingered around her waist as he looked her up and down. She gave him a quick peck on his cheek before they departed and she was certain she noticed him blush.

Soon Rachel purposely began showing up in places where she was certain to run into Milo. She showed off her leaner body in tight designer jeans, and fitted O State t-shirts. Milo noticed the other guys noticing Rachel. While his heart was true to Bianca, who was at home waiting for him, Rachel was there in flesh and blood. He could not resist returning Rachel's stares, hugs and sweet kisses. The more Rachel and Milo found themselves together, the more he gave into her feminine wiles.

By the time summer vacation rolled around, Rachel was sure she had her hooks sufficiently into Milo to keep him away from Bianca. Rachel returned home with Rev. and Mrs. Pettigrew and for the first week she sat in her bedroom and waited for Milo's call. Each time the doorbell rang, Rachel ran to the door, practically knocking over Mrs. Pettigrew on her way. Friends from high school stopped by to visit, including Kelli, but their contact and friendship fell short. She desperately wanted to see Milo. Their chance meeting occurred on the second Sunday of summer vacation. Milo walked right into Rev. Pettigrew's Sunday morning service with Bianca Goode on his arm.

Chapter 40

Bianca

Watching her best friend Kelli walk down the aisle, Bianca imagined herself becoming Mrs. Milo McFadden. She, like Kelli, did not know who would walk her down the aisle. It certainly would not be Mr. Goode. Bianca would walk by herself down the aisle if she had to in order to get to Milo.

Her life lately consisted of sitting in her little efficiency apartment each day after working as a cashier at the local grocery store. She watched television each week night and every Saturday night she went out with a group of girls from work, who liked to get high. Bianca enjoyed getting high from booze and weed and never missed their Saturday night outings. On Sundays, Milo called collect. She could barely pay the mounting telephone bill, in addition to her rent and bus fare. Yet, she held on. Beauty school would be starting soon and things would get much better after that. Then she would have a job that she enjoyed. More importantly, she would be able to afford a car and could drive to visit Milo.

In the meantime, she waited for him, patiently. She rejected all offers for dates from her co-workers and other guys who came through her line at the supermarket. She was Milo McFadden's girlfriend and she was true to him. She just hoped he was doing the same.

* * * *

"Do you regret not going to college?" Bianca asked Kelli as they sat across from one another at Ryan's steakhouse.

"Sometimes, but mostly I enjoy my job. I mean, I don't want to do clerical work forever. So I am going to start taking classes at the Kelly School of Business soon. They said my acceptance into the school is good for one year. It's just going to be hard paying for it, now that Greg's out of work."

"Kelly I didn't know. Why didn't you say something? You didn't have to take me out for my birthday. I could've waited."

"It's no problem," Kelli said and reached across the table and held her friend's hand. "I knew you were a little down, since Milo couldn't come home this weekend. Plus, I borrowed some money from Rita to pay the rent this month."

"What's Greg going to do about a job?"

"He said he's been looking. He'll get something soon."

"Well, if he's interested, we're hiring at the market where I work. It only pays minimum wage, but it's something until he finds another job."

"Thanks, Bianca. I'll let him know."

"What about your mother-in-law? How's she acting these days?"

"I don't know what to say about that woman. Last month she took Greg out to dinner for his birthday, just the two of them. He said they needed some 'bonding time'. She had him all to herself for eighteen years. How much more 'bonding time' is she going to need with her son? I don't understand her and I don't understand him sometimes either."

Bianca smiled, "Don't worry. He'll grow up soon. Guys mature slower than we do. He'll see his mother for who she really is soon enough."

"She's going to have to accept the fact that we're married now. We're not just high school boyfriend and girlfriend anymore. We're a family. She'll never accept us if he doesn't put his foot down with her antics. I wonder what she's going to do when we have kids?"

Bianca dropped her fork, "Are you trying to tell me something."

"No way! Not yet!" We're waiting until I finish college and Greg gets a steady job. But, we are enjoying the practice!"

The two friends squealed and then the topic of conversation turned to sex. The temperature got hotter at their table than the kitchen inside Ryan's steakhouse.

Chapter 41

Staking The Lot

Anybody who was anybody was going to celebrate New Year's Eve at Faces nightclub in Dayton, Ohio. It was the newest and best nightclub closest to Fairfield. Kelli had talked Bianca and Rachel into reserving a table together. Neither Rachel nor Bianca wanted to sit at a table with the other. Still, Kelli insisted they were all friends and since they were all going to be at the same nightclub anyway, they may as well sit together. Besides, if you didn't reserve a table, you were likely to be sitting way in the back in the open seating. Reluctantly, Rachel and Bianca agreed. So it was settled Kelli and Greg would be attending, Bianca and Milo, and Rachel with friends from Ohio State.

Bianca and Milo were already at the reserved table alone, when Kelli and Greg arrived. They were both sipping on drinks. Bianca had an umbrella in her glass. Milo looked handsome in a dark suit and Bianca looked classic in a short black dress that hung off her shoulders. Kelli and Greg greeted them both and Kelli excused herself right away and left in search of the restroom. Bianca noticed the strain on Kelli's face and followed behind her.

"What's wrong?" Bianca asked, half-shouting above the music when she caught up with Kelli.

Kelli wiped her eyes with a tissue. "Girl, we got into a fight on the way here."

"What happened?" Bianca asked.

"Greg just told me he lost his job again. Every time I look up, he loses his job. I've had the same job for three years and he's been through more than ten jobs. He can't hold onto a job for more than a couple of months and he always does something to get fired! But he always says it's not his fault! Bianca, I'm not sure how much of this I can take!"

"Calm down, Sweetie," Bianca said and wrapped her arms around Kelli. Then Bianca reached inside her purse and brought out several bills all wrapped together. She stuffed the bills inside Kelli's hand tightly.

"No. You don't have to do that Bianca, really."

"Look, it's just for a few drinks tonight. I want you to have a good time tonight, Kelli.

Besides, I make good tips on my job. Look at me. This is a designer dress from Saks Fifth Avenue!" Bianca stood back and twirled around so Kelli could get a good look at her dress.

"Wow! And it looks good on you, too!"

"Come on, Girl. Wipe your face and let's get out there and have a good time!"

Kelli tucked the bills inside her purse, wiped her face and touched up her make up. She looked pretty good, too. Her dress had come from JC Penny, but it was still cute on her.

Kelli and Bianca walked back toward their reserved table. Just as they had left them, their guys were sitting at the table, but Rachel and a few of her female friends had arrived. Rachel was sitting on Milo's lap, laughing, and he was smiling and talking to the others. Kelli almost didn't recognize Rachel, she was as thin as a supermodel, and her hair was all cut off and tapered in the back. Whether Bianca recognized Rachel or not, she clearly saw another woman sitting on her man's lap and she stormed right up to the table.

"Rachel, get your ass up off my man!" Bianca shouted above the music.

Some of the other partygoers near the table turned around to see the commotion. Milo stood up so fast, Rachel slid right off his lap. If Rachel had not been so quick on her feet, she would have crash-landed to the floor.

Milo approached Bianca. "It's cool, B," he said, holding out his hands. "Come on. She didn't mean anything by it?"

Bianca continued to shout. "How do you know she didn't mean anything by it? She was sitting on your lap, wasn't she?"

"Come on, B. We were just all sitting around and joking," Milo tried to explain.

"All the empty seats at this table and she had to sit on your lap?"

Everyone else sat back and watched the drama, except Rachel, the one who started it all. She approached Milo and Bianca only with the intention of antagonizing Bianca.

"Bianca, we were just talking about something that happened at O State. There's no reason to get all upset. The rest of us are just chilling out and having a good time. Doing hair all day is making you boring."

Bianca lunged out at Rachel, but Milo grabbed her hands just in the nick of time.

"Stay away from me and my man, Rachel! I'm not playing with you!"

Rachel threw her head back and laughed. Then she spoke seductively, "I'll see you back at O State, Milo."

Milo didn't look back in Rachel's direction. He kept his focus and his hands on Bianca. He knew if he let Bianca go, she'd go after Rachel for sure.

Rachel and her crew walked away and sat at another table for the evening.

Greg whispered to Kelli, "Milo has his ass in a sling! If Bianca doesn't scratch Rachel's eyes out in here, I bet she's gonna scratch his out on the way home."

Kelli was in no mood to poke fun at the deteriorating relationship between her two best friends. This had been her last ditch effort to get her friends together. She had hoped they could sit at the same table and ring in the New Year together. Now that wasn't going to happen, and she feared Rachel and Bianca were destined to remain enemies from that point on. She looked at her husband and commented dryly, "You should stay out of it, Greg. You should be worried about me scratching your eyes out!"

Greg looked at Kelli innocently. "But I didn't do anything. Nobody was sitting on my lap!"

"Just shut up, Greg," Kelli said weakly. "Here," she handed Greg two of the bills from Bianca. "Go buy us all a round of drinks."

Kelli, Greg, Bianca and Milo tried their best to have a good time for the remainder of the night. A few other friends from Fairfield joined them and soon their table was filled. Drinks, chicken wings and party favors were passed around just in time for the countdown to midnight. It seemed their evening out had not been a waste of time after all.

Yet as Milo returned to the bar later for more drinks, Rachel walked up and planted a long and passionate New Year's kiss on his lips. Milo knew he was dead wrong when he slipped Rachel some tongue action in return.

Chapter 42
Kelli

Kelli planned on waiting until after she finished Business College before she and Greg started a family, but babies came when they wanted to, not necessarily when they were planned. She sat on the bathroom floor crying and staring at the plus sign on the stick of the home pregnancy test. A million things ran across her mind. She thought they had no money for doctor's bills, maternity clothes, a two-bedroom apartment, a crib, diapers, formula or a babysitter. The more she thought about it the sooner the list was longer than a ten year-old's Christmas wish list.

Thankfully Greg walked into the bathroom and interrupted her thoughts before she suffered a complete nervous breakdown on the floor. He took one look at the home pregnancy test and his wife sitting on the floor in tears. Greg wasn't as sharp as a tack, but he was able to put two and two together and come up with four. Immediately, he sank to the floor and wrapped his arms around Kelli lovingly.

"Why didn't you tell me you thought you were pregnant?"

"I wanted to be certain. I was hoping it wasn't true."

Kelli looked up at Greg and saw the feeling of hurt in his face. "Not yet. I just didn't want to be pregnant yet. I wanted to wait until I was done with Business College."

"Yeah, I know this isn't the best time, but I'm here, Kelli, and I'm not leaving. I'll never leave you. Not like my father left me."

"I know you're not leaving, Greg. I just wanted the timing to be right. We're still just getting on our feet."

"Come on," he said. Greg helped his wife up from the floor. Before she could discard the contents of the home pregnancy test, Greg reached for the stick and stared at the blue plus sign.

Kelli wanted to warn him that she had peed all over that stick only minutes ago.

Greg said, "It's blue—that means it's a boy, right!"

Kelli wanted to tell him the sign was blue regardless. There was a plus sign if you were pregnant and a minus sign if you were not. Yet, she decided as long as it made Greg happy, she would go along with it.

"Yes, that's exactly what it means. We're going to have a boy!"

Greg picked Kelli up and twirled her around and around. She had never seen him so animated and so happy. He jumped up and down on the bed and ran around their tiny apartment. Then, most surprisingly, he ran to the telephone and dialed it.

"Hey, Ma, guess what? Me and Kelli are having a baby. And it's a boy!"

Kelli knew Patty Campbell's face just cracked on the other end of the telephone.

* * * *

Almost immediately, Greg went out and picked up a second job. He worked nearly day and night. Kelli hardly ever saw him between her full-time job and night class. Still, she was happy to have a husband who was finally showing some initiative. Their rent was caught up, they were paying the monthly doctor bills and they had extra money in the bank. It was a relief to Kelli not to feel like she had the weight of the world on her shoulders. Greg even surprised her further by cooking breakfast each morning. Even more shocking was that he said his mother suggested to him how important it was to feed Kelli a good breakfast every morning now that she was expecting. So each morning he prepared some of her favorite foods: scrambled eggs, waffles, pancakes, French toast and there was always a tall glass of orange juice on the side. Kelli was in heaven.

* * * *

Patty Campbell refused to let Kelli think she was coming between her and her son, Greg. The minute Greg told her Kelli was pregnant; Patty knew Kelli was trying to trap her innocent son in a dead-end marriage. Although she was a good Christian woman, Patty knew things. She knew evil things. Her Auntie Helen had lived in New Orleans for more than twenty years and she was a well-known Voodoo Priestess. After Patty's husband, Peter, left her with an infant son to raise, Patty brought Peter's hair brush to Auntie Helen. Just like in the movies, Auntie Helen fashioned a voodoo doll using Peter's hair. Peter didn't die, but Patty made sure he wished he had. Auntie Helen made Peter blind in one eye, crippled in one leg and his organ no longer functioned. He would not get another woman pregnant and leave her to raise a child all alone.

Patty drove to Auntie Helen's house in Blue Ash and asked her for a potion. Something that would make a woman miscarry her unborn child. Auntie Helen said that was easy. Patty could have used a combination of store bought aids to make up that kind of concoction. Still, Auntie Helen mixed a potion for Patty anyway. She reached inside her own medicine cabinet for ingredients and then reached under her bathroom sink and added something she used to clean her toilet. She handed a small black bottle to Patty. Auntie Helen was not above charging Patty for the potion and Patty was obliged to pay.

Patty invited both Greg and Kelli for dinner for the first time in their marriage. She was certain to separate Kelli's drink from Greg's.

* * * *

When Kelli miscarried she was greatly saddened. The unfortunate experience was both mentally and physically depleting. Rita and Bianca were by her side offering her support. Yet, Greg remained distant. Greg was devastated. He never got over it and he blamed Kelli for losing his son.

Chapter 43
Rachel

News of Milo McFadden's position as a second-round NFL draft pick spread throughout the Ohio State campus like wild fire. When the good news reached Rachel, she was dually pulled, excited for what an NFL career meant for her and Milo's life together, yet panicked because she had not yet secured her relationship with Milo. It was her senior year and she realized it probably meant her last chance to get Milo. So, her closest girlfriend, Paris, rallied behind her.

Paris Cunningham had been Rachel's best friend on campus since their freshman year. She was popular on campus, attractive and had a steady boyfriend. Rachel had confided everything in Paris. She knew Rachel had been desperately pursuing Milo since their first year on campus.

Also, Paris knew Milo had confessed his love to his girlfriend waiting for him at home. Paris had the opportunity to see Bianca in action New Year's Eve when they attended Faces nightclub. She saw for herself how rude and stuck up Bianca Goode could be. How dare she act like Milo McFadden was her personal property, when they all hung out with Milo and his crew on a regular basis?

There was no way Rachel and Paris were going to let Bianca Goode beat Rachel out on becoming Milo McFadden's woman, the newest NFL player. Rachel had told her all about Bianca. About Bianca's biracial heritage and how she thought she was better than the other black girls in Fairfield, because she had long hair and fair skin. She also told her that Bianca was promiscuous and had a bad reputation in their hometown. Together, they decided Rachel needed to devise a written game plan. They agreed sneaking little kisses and hugs from Milo was mere child's play. Now Rachel had to pull out the big guns.

Paris brought beer for their meeting and she popped one open and poured the contents into two Styrofoam cups. Once the beer began to take effect and free-flowing thoughts were spurred, the young ladies were ready to get down to the business of developing an iron-clad plan.

"Are you ready to do some real grown-up antics to get your man?" Paris asked.

Rachel giggled, but nodded her head yes. She was ready all right. She would attempt to walk on water or part the Red Sea if she thought it would help her land Milo.

Paris lay back on Rachel's bed and stared at the ceiling in deep thought.

"First, you have to stop wasting your time on all these other losers on this campus and focus in on Milo. When other guys try to talk to you, let them know straight up, you're Milo's lady," Paris suggested.

"But...practically everyone knows Milo has a girlfriend back home," Rachel protested.

"Now everyone's going to know Milo has a girlfriend on campus. It will keep the other females at bay. I don't think there are too many girls on this campus who want to contend with you. You have a reputation for kicking butt and taking names later!"

Rachel listed: *Tell other guys I'm Milo's girl.*

"What do I do if the story gets back to Milo?" Rachel asked.

"You want it to get back to Milo. Let him know you are his woman for the taking. Make yourself completely open and available to him. Trying to make him jealous with other guys hasn't worked the past three years. This is it, Girl. You have to take a stand!"

Rachel took in a deep breath and said, "Okay. I can do this. What else?"

"Get your hands on his letterman jacket and wear it to the homecoming football game and around campus."

"And how am I going to get my hands on his letterman jacket!"

"You never heard of stealing something, silly girl? He lives on the first floor of his dorm. Try climbing in the window or jimmying the lock. "

"Okay. *Get his letterman jacket.*"

"Oh yeah—while you're in there, gather his laundry and wash and fold it up for him and leave a little note, *Love, Rachel.*"

Rachel didn't like that idea of doing domestic work, "Why don't I get on my hands and knees and scrub his dorm room floor while I'm at it," she said sarcastically.

"That's the spirit, Rachel. You're really getting into it now!"

Rachel could hardly believe Paris wanted her to stoop so low, but this was Milo McFadden they were talking about and she would do anything. So she wrote: B*reak into his dorm room, do laundry, clean his dorm room and steal his jacket.*

"Buy him something. Guys like it when a woman buys them things."

"Like, what kind of things?"

"Clothes, jewelry, shoes, sexy underwear. Make it a big production. Wrap it up in glitzy gift paper."

"There goes my charge card balance," Rachel stated flatly.

"Just think about all the things he'll be buying for you when he's playing in the NFL."

Rachel smiled and said, "I've got it. She wrote: *Buy him gifts.*"

"As a matter of fact, have flowers delivered to his dorm room, congratulating him on his recent good news."

"Got it. *Send flowers.*

"Do something nice for his family."

"Yes. That'll be easy his mom is the secretary for my dad's church. And his little brother, Maurice, he's a senior at Fairfield High. That should be easy to do something nice for the two of them? Real easy!"

"You have to buddy up to his family. Do something nice for his mother and brother. Something they'll tell Milo about. It will definitely impress Milo."

Rachel wrote: D*o something nice for Milo's family.* She was unsure just what to do, but she would figure it out.

Paris thought intently. "There's no way around it. You're going to have to get him into bed."

"I know, I know. I've been trying since our freshman year," Rachel said exasperated.

Paris sat up and took a long swig of beer. She refilled her cup and returned to her thinking position. "I know! I saw a movie. A woman wanted to seduce a man. She showed up at his place with nothing on except a rain coat and a pair of high heels."

Rachel was no prude. She had put her birth control pills to good use on the O State campus, but showing up booty-butt naked was something entirely different.

"Wow! Paris, I don't know about that one."

"Come on, Rachel. You have to pull out all the stops. This year is your last chance. If you don't get him now, you may lose him to Bianca forever."

"You're right," Rachel contended. She wrote: *Show up with nothing on but a rain coat and high heeled shoes.*

* * * *

Rachel put her credit card to good use and ordered a dozen red roses to be delivered to Milo's dorm room. The gesture yielded a positive result. Milo picked up the telephone immediately and thanked her profusely. He admitted no one had ever sent him flowers before and he thought it was *sexy.* Rachel liked his choice of words. That's exactly what she wanted him to think of when he thought of her *sexy.*

Getting into Milo's dorm room was not as easy as Paris and Rachel imagined. Milo didn't have a private room like Rachel's. So, not only did Rachel have to be concerned with Milo catching her, but she had to also be concerned about his roommate, Jerry. There was just no other way around it: since Milo stayed in the athletic dorm, attempt a break in, during a home football game. Everyone would certainly be at the game. So they waited and made their move. They tried the window, but it was locked, tight and secure. They tried three windows before they found one that was unlocked. They climbed inside, walked through some doors and were quickly in the hallway. They made a beeline to Milo's room. Paris went to work on the lock with a bobby pin, then a metal fingernail file.

"I've almost got it," Paris revealed, and then dug into her backpack for a tool with a long, pointy, metal end.

"Where did you get that thing?" Bianca asked.

"I stole it from the janitor's closet."

Rachel could not believe Paris had *stolen* a tool, so they could *break into* Milo's room. She was certainly glad Paris was on her side. Paris was the kind of girl who could get things done.

They were in.

Paris grabbed Milo's laundry and headed to the basement with a pocket full of quarters to wash, dry and fold Milo's clothing and linens. Rachel busied herself with cleaning the entire dorm room. She gathered up two empty pizza boxes, a half-dozen soda cans, and greasy napkins spread about, and emptied the overflowing waste basket. She didn't dust a picture of Bianca that Milo had sitting on his desk. Instead, she placed the frame face down in the top drawer of Milo's desk.

When the room was clean and Milo's laundry complete, Rachel grabbed Milo's letterman jacket, left a simple note sprayed with her favorite perfume, *Love Rachel.* They exited the building as quickly as possible, laughing all the way back to their own room.

This time when Milo called to thank her, he invited her out to dinner. He said that was the kindest thing anyone had ever done for him. She grinned and changed the subject at dinner when he asked her just how she had gotten inside his room. She admitted to borrowing his letterman jacket, when he asked about it. She was glad he never mentioned the picture of Bianca.

****

Homecoming weekend would be an excessive time for celebration, good cheer and hot steamy love. At least Rachel hoped for the hot steamy love. She proudly wore Milo's letterman jacket to the big game and was pleased as punch when she ran into Bianca as they both made their way to the bleachers to take a seat. Bianca clearly recognized Milo's jacket right off. Her temper boiled immediately. It was evident, because her fair complexion turned beet-red.

Ironically, it was homecoming night that put the icing on the cake. Rachel called Milo and asked if he would be in his room long enough for her to return his jacket. He certainly wanted to wear it that evening, when he went out with his buddies. Rachel bribed a group of freshman girls, who were hosting a small celebration in their dorm, to entice Milo's roommate, Jerry, to attend their party. She paid them handsomely in cash and beer. She sat in her car outside Milo's dorm and waited for his unsuspecting roommate to leave with the young girls. Rachel stepped out of her car, wearing nothing more than a raincoat and a pair of stilettos. She sashayed right up to Milo's dorm room. When he opened the door, she stepped inside.

"Oh, I forgot your letterman jacket. Silly me," she blushed. She turned and shut the door behind her and securely locked it. "But I did bring you this," she said and opened the raincoat wide, revealing her toned, long, lean and completely naked body.

Milo took full advantage of what Rachel offered.

Chapter 44
Bianca

During Christmas break, the relationship between Milo and Bianca had clearly changed. He was distant. Their conversation was strained and their love-making was awkward. Milo and Bianca had been passionate lovers for years, and it was evident something was bothering him. Bianca tried her best to keep her disappointment to herself, but her strange demeanor was apparent to anyone who knew her.

"Hey, Girl, what's the matter?" Kelli asked Bianca as they sat on the sofa in Kelli's apartment.

"I think me and Milo are having problems," Bianca said, hanging her head. "I've been waiting for him all of this time. I've been stuck in this hellacious little town, because he didn't want me to be far from him. I've sacrificed everything."

"You guys are nearly at the finish line now. Hold on. His graduation is just a few months away. He'll be drafted by the NFL and you guys will be off, leaving me here in this God-forsaken place," Kelli teased.

"I'm trying to hang on, but it's hard," Bianca stated seriously. "I didn't tell you this, but when I went to his homecoming football game, I ran into Rachel in the stands."

"Oh, brother, don't tell me you guys got into it."

"No, we didn't get into it, but Rachel was wearing Milo's letterman jacket."

Kelli tried to think quickly. She knew Rachel had been trying to come between Bianca and Milo, but she had to say something to minimize the damage. "Look, Bianca, don't make too much of it. Rachel is Milo's home girl and that's it. We all graduated from high school together. I know you and Rachel aren't really friends anymore, but Milo would never...she would never..." Kelli couldn't find the words to finish smoothing things over.

"I wouldn't put anything past Rachel. We were friends once and I know how evil and devious she can be."

"Really, Bianca, I wouldn't worry about that. Besides, what did Milo have to say about it?"

"He said Rachel *borrowed* his jacket."

"Well, there you go. No harm, no foul. You and I borrow each other's jewelry and purses all the time. I'd borrow your clothes if you weren't such a midget." Kelli tried to make light of the situation.

Bianca finally smiled, "All right, *Too Tall Kelli Brown. Excuse me! Kelli Brown-Campbell.*"

Together Bianca and Kelli enjoyed a laugh. Still, in the back of Kelli's mind she knew Rachel was up to no good. Rachel had to know Bianca would never miss Milo's big homecoming game. She knew Rachel had worn Milo's letterman jacket purposely on that day. She had half a mind to call Rachel and give her a piece of her mind. Yet, on the other hand, she didn't want to stoke any flames if they weren't there. Instead, she sat back and hoped for all their sakes that things were not as they appeared. She hoped Milo hadn't bitten Rachel's bait.

Bianca thought Kelli may have known more than she revealed. Still, she tried to wipe the thought out of her mind. Kelli was her only real friend. Her so-called family was nearly non-existent since she had moved out after high school. Her sister, Lilly, had to sneak to even talk to Bianca on the telephone. Mr. Goode had said Bianca was dead to him. As if she had ever done anything to him!

Chapter 45
Clearing and Excavating

Fairfield was truly a small town and one was bound to see everyone they knew at any public event. The annual Fairfield carnival was just that way. Rita and Kelli had gone each year since Kelli was a child and this year would be no exception. Kelli and Greg would meet Rita and Able there.

Kelli sat on a bench munching on pink cotton candy, while Greg stood in line to purchase ride tickets. He knew Kelli didn't enjoy the rides, but he had stopped doing much with her anyway and figured he would hang out with Able when he arrived. Soon Kelli spotted Rita and Able coming through the entrance gate and she met them and greeted them both with a hug.

As predicted, Greg and Able went ahead of the others, while Rita and Kelli walked slowly behind. Rita and Kelli wrapped their arms around one another's waists as they walked, took in the small town crowd and braved the cool spring breeze. When the cotton candy was finished, Rita and Kelli shared a huge fresh pretzel.

All the while, the group waved and greeted old neighbors, old classmates and old church members. Fairfield was truly a small town. So, it was no surprise when their group bumped into Bianca and Milo. Bianca was enjoying an elephant ear as Milo busied himself with a basketball stand at one of the game booths.

Rita and Kelli hugged Bianca and said it was nice to see her out and enjoying herself. Kelli and Bianca had not seen each other recently. Kelli took Bianca by the arm and ushered her away from the others.

"It seems everything is going okay between the two of you."

"Not really," Bianca frowned. "I had to drag him out today. He said he didn't feel like going out today. That he didn't feel like being around a crowd."

"Well, he'd better get used to it. He's going to be a big NFL star this fall."

Bianca looked lovingly in Milo's direction, "Yeah. This fall everything's going to change."

Kelli and Bianca headed back to the group just in time for Milo to hand Bianca a huge white bear with a red heart in the center. Bianca smiled and accepted the bear.

Everyone hung around Milo, congratulating him on his NFL accomplishment. Milo was modest. He averted their attention by handing a few bills to the booth attendant and said, "I'll win one for you now, Kelli."

Kelli smiled and said, "Thanks, because I haven't so much as touched a basketball since high school. My skills are rusty."

Everyone laughed.

Within minutes Milo sank every ball and reached up and selected a gigantic pink bear for Kelli. Kelli grabbed the bear with one arm and placed her empty arm around Milo's neck.

"Thanks, Milo," she said genuinely.

Kelli shared a hopeful look with Bianca and then the group parted, proceeding to the next game booth.

As Kelli looked into the crowd she spotted Rachel at a distance. Kelli told Rita she'd be right back and took off in Rachel's direction. As she approached, Kelli could see a fierce scowl on Rachel's face.

"Hello, traitor," Rachel said harshly, folding her arms.

"Wait just one minute," Kelli protested. "You have no right."

"I have every right!" Rachel responded. "You know how I feel about Milo. How could you, Kelli? You're supposed to be my friend. How could you stand over there and talk to that girl?"

"That girl," Kelli reminded her, "is our friend and her name is Bianca. She's the same *girl* that Milo has been with since high school. The one that he took to the prom, the one that he promised to marry when he gets out of school..."

Rachel cut her off. "The one that I'll kill before I let her have my man!" Rachel screamed. With one sudden angry motion, Rachel turned around and walked into the crowd.

Kelli knew Rachel was in trouble. She was obviously completely out of her mind. The Rachel that she had just encountered was not the Rachel she had grown up next door with. Rachel, the child, had been a brat; but Rachel, the grown up, was a woman possessed.

Chapter 46
Kelli

It had literally been years since Kelli and Greg had been intimate. She knew following her miscarriage that there had been a change in her young marriage, but she hoped and prayed that time would heal her relationship with her husband. It had not.

They lived their lives more like roommates than a committed couple in love. They had been passionately in love in the beginning, but the spark had long ago flickered out. Kelli spent more and more time at work. As her career blossomed, she decided to build upon the two-year business degree she had earned, and apply for a four-year degree at a local community college.

"So, what do you think?" she asked Greg, trying to get his opinion about her returning to school as they sat across from one another at their kitchen table.

"It's your money and your time," Greg responded flatly.

Kelli drew in a deep breath. It was getting more difficult to have a conversation with Greg and he was really trying her patience.

"Going back to school will be expensive, so, of course, we'll have to cut back on our spending. Plus, it'll mean attending class late into the evening."

Greg sat in silence and chewed his food. He averted eye contact.

"Greg, if you have an opinion, I'd really like to hear it," Kelli insisted.

"I just don't see the point," He said flatly, and rose from the table. He grabbed his plate from the table and headed to the sofa to plant himself in front of the TV.

Kelli instinctively jumped up from the table. "You don't see the point in what? Me going back to school or us talking about it?"

"Either," he said from the sofa.

Kelli marched into the living room and planted herself squarely in front of the TV, completely blocking Greg's view.

"What's your problem, Greg?" she shouted.

"I don't have a problem. It's you that has a problem." Now he looked her into the eye. "You want to waste money and time going back to school when you already have a decent job. It's just stupid."

"Stupid." Kelli said, placing both hands on her hips. "Getting my bachelor's degree is stupid?"

Greg stood to his feet. "Yes, that's what I said stupid!

Before Kelli said it, she knew she would live to regret it. "Stupid is losing a job every three or four months, because you're too lazy to get up out of bed and get there on time!"

"I never lost a job because of being late!"

"I see you walk out the house late almost every morning. If not because you're late, then tell me why, Greg. Why do you always manage to lose your job?"

Greg stuttered and stammered. Then he blurted, "Because the man don't want to see a black man get ahead. That's why."

Kelli leaned her head back and laughed. "The man? It's the man. That's the best you can come up with?"

"It's the truth," Greg said, and returned to his seat on the sofa. "You wouldn't understand. The only reason you got that job you have is because of Able."

"Able may have helped me get the job, but I'm the one who has kept it. I get to work on time every morning, I work hard and I work until the job is done. I went to Business College and earned a two-year degree at the same time. What have you done to improve yourself, Greg?"

Greg rolled his eyes at Kelli and looked through her at the television.

"That's what I thought," she said. Kelli turned and walked out of the room. She shouted defiantly from the kitchen, "And I'm registering for classes tomorrow!"

Later Kelli locked herself into their bedroom. She sat staring at the ceiling half the night. She made up her mind that when she heard Greg attempt to turn the door knob, she would let him inside. He never tried to enter their room all night. Greg had no desire to join Kelli in their bed.

Chapter 47
Rachel

Milo was cheating on Bianca with Rachel. He was also cheating on Rachel with another girl off-campus. Rachel knew this because she followed Milo everywhere he traveled. Tonya Martin was a junior in Milo's Advanced Economics class. It seemed Tonya prepared home-cooked meals for Milo and served up dessert in her bedroom. Rachel had to get rid of her.

At first, Rachel sent anonymous death threats through the mail to scare Tonya. Then she wrote in red paint on her apartment door "Die Bitch." Finally, she called Paris for assistance to deliver the final threat.

Paris' skills at breaking in were invaluable. They would hit Tonya's apartment in the cover of night. The stakes would be much higher than entering into Milo's dorm room to do him the favor of cleaning and doing his laundry. This time, Rachel and Paris were committing a real felony. So they dressed the part. They wore dark clothing, ski masks and gloves. Rachel wore black leather gloves and Paris, like a fool, wore black wool mittens.

They broke into the apartment and trashed it severely. Rachel went straight for the bedroom and was determined to destroy the mattress. At first sight of the place where she knew her man was doing another woman, her first instinct was to set the bed on fire. She was crazy in love, but she was no arsonist. She ripped the blanket and sheets off the bed and then headed straight for the kitchen and brought out a knife. She butchered the mattress. Next, they stabbed the sofa and loveseat with knives, leaving the inner cushions spilling out.

When Paris discovered a bottle of bleach under the kitchen sink she instinctively decided to dump all the clothes from the closet and drawers into the bathtub. She dumped the bottle of bleach on them, ruining everything. Rachel headed back to the kitchen and dumped food and drinks all over the living room carpet. They turned over the kitchen chairs and table and knocked down the few pictures on the wall.

As Rachel and Paris rushed to depart the obliterated apartment, Rachel took one final look back over her shoulder, satisfied with what she saw.

In the aftermath, "Thelma and Louise" were successful in scaring Tonya. Milo's off-campus mistress moved out of the apartment immediately and back into a door room with three other girls. She had no privacy. The open invitation for Milo to spend the night was closed.

Chapter 48
Bianca

"If this is some kind of joke, Milo, I don't find it funny at all!" Bianca shouted through the telephone. "You can't seriously be breaking up with me after I waited four years for you…don't tell me it's over now… no, don't say it… Rachel Pettigrew…you must be out of your mind!"

Tears poured from Bianca's eyes. She could hardly believe what she was hearing. She sat all alone, exactly how her life had been for the past four years. She had been committed to waiting for Milo McFadden. Four long years of only spending school breaks together, coupled with an occasional visit in Columbus. She had been true to him, despite all the other viable offers she had received. Now, in return for her loyalty, she was being kicked in the teeth. Not once, but twice.

Milo was leaving her. For Rachel Pettigrew! Devious Rachel had been successful in stealing Milo from her. He had called Bianca on the telephone to tell her so. He didn't even have the courage or respect for Bianca to tell her in person. She could still hear Milo's voice on the other end of the telephone, and she wanted it all to stop. Besides, the call was on her dime. Milo had called collect.

Just as he said, "I hope we can still be friends," Bianca slammed the phone down on the hook. She hoped it burst Milo's ear drum. She sat and cried alone for hours before she found the strength to call Kelli, but her friend wasn't home. Greg reminded her that Kelli would be in class until 9 p.m.

Chapter 49
Framing

Rachel groveled to Kelli. "It would mean so much to me if you would be one of my bridesmaids. I know this is short notice, but we've been friends since we were kids and I've always dreamed that you would be in my wedding," she said brightly.

Kelli starred at Rachel blankly. "Rachel Pettigrew, you have all the nerve in the world. The last time I saw you, you called me a *traitor*."

"I'm sorry about that," Rachel said, trying to appear remorseful. "I really mean it. I was in a bad place at the time. You just don't know how hard it was on me." Rachel paused. "Milo and I were in love, but Bianca had some kind of wicked hold on him and wouldn't let him go."

"No, I think the only wicked one in the group is you," Kelli said dryly.

"Come on, Kelli. We're not kids anymore. When Milo and I went to Ohio State together we fell in love. It was no silly high school romance. We weren't kids anymore. What he had with *her* was already over by then. *She* was his past and I'm his future. Now we're getting married next month, before he goes off to training camp and I want you to be in my wedding."

"I don't know, Rachel; it is short notice," Kelli said and looked away.

"There's something else you should know, Kelli."

Kelli looked Rachel in the eye.

"I'm pregnant."

"What! Rachel, don't tell me you've gone and gotten yourself pregnant by Milo on purpose. What happened to the birth control pills you started taking when we were back in high school!"

"Nothing's one hundred percent effective," Rachel said in her defense. "Don't forget, you got pregnant on the pill, too."

"I was married," Kelli reminded her friend. "I was a virgin until my wedding night."

"Well, not everyone can be a saint like you."

Kelli sighed heavily.

Kelli couldn't deny it. She and Rachel had been friends forever. Through the years she had suffered through the good, bad and ugly with Rachel. She didn't approve of Rachel's marriage to

Milo, but they were two adults who had made a decision. Now a baby was on the way. Kelli looked into Rachel's eyes and saw the girl she knew long ago—a brat, who always got what she wanted.

"Okay. I'll do it, but you'd better not pick an ugly bridesmaid's dress," Kelli teased.

Rachel said, "No uglier than the dress I wore for your wedding."

They laughed and it was almost like old times.

* * * *

Kelli rushed out the apartment to her car with the hideous kelly-green bridesmaid's dress, covered in plastic, draped over one arm. She also had a bag filled with shoes and accessories for the dress hanging over the same shoulder. Her purse was hung on the opposite shoulder and she held her car keys in her hand. Kelli was weighed down and struggled to get to her car. Before she could make it there, she was met by Bianca.

"Hey, Bianca." Kelli awkwardly tried to hug Bianca, but the wedding paraphernalia in her arms made it nearly impossible.

Bianca noticed the dress. Seeing it only cut deep through her heart. "So, I see you're on your way to the church," Bianca said sadly.

Kelli could see Bianca had been crying and she felt horrible. "Yeah. Hey, I'm sorry, Bianca, that we haven't talked. It's just that I've been so busy with work and school."

"I understand. I know how it is," Bianca responded.

An awkward silence fell between them.

"I just stopped by to let you know I'm leaving."

"Leaving? Where are you going?"

"A co-worker has a good lead on a job in Los Angeles. Hair and make-up are big business in L.A. so I'm going west to make my fortune," Bianca tried to say with some enthusiasm, but her voice shook with nervousness.

"Of course, L.A. is a great place to do hair and make-up." Kelli paused. "I bet you'll make a lot of money out there."

"Yeah. So, I better get going. I just wanted you to know."

Kelli and Bianca hugged and crushed the revolting green dress Kelli would be wearing at Rachel's and Milo's wedding.

"Bianca, I'm so sorry," Kelli said during their embrace.

Tears ran down Bianca's face and she said, "I'll call you when I get there." Then she walked away lifelessly to her car, got inside and drove away.

* * * *

When Kelli arrived at the church, she walked into an unexpected display of drama by Rachel. All six bridesmaids stood around whispering in hushed tones. Kelli walked past two young ladies who whispered the words "shot gun wedding," and then ran into three others. One of them said, "No wonder she won't come out." Finally, someone officially announced Rachel was locked inside the bathroom down the hall and was refusing to come out. Kelli walked down the hall and witnessed Mrs. Pettigrew standing outside the bathroom door, knocking softly.

"Rachel, Honey. It's okay. It's perfectly natural to be a bit nervous on your wedding day. Come on out, Sweetie. It'll be okay."

Mrs. Pettigrew looked up and saw Kelli walking towards her. She was elated; Rachel had been asking for Kelli.

"Rachel, Kelli's here. I'm sending her inside. Now, open the door."

Kelli barely had time to fully digest what was happening, before Mrs. Pettigrew took her by the arm forcefully and jammed her against the door, before Rachel could unlock it. When the bathroom door opened, Kelli could hardly believe how Rachel appeared. Rachel quickly reached her arm out, grabbed Kelli inside and slammed the door shut again.

Kelli looked in awe at Rachel. Her best friend since childhood was the most beautiful bride she had ever seen before in her life. Rachel's beautiful dark skin against the pure white dress was an amazing and beautiful contrast. Rachel's make-up was impeccable. She looked like a black Barbie doll and Kelli could only stare into Rachel's eyes.

Rachel's eyes were wide when she whispered, "Kelli, I've gone and really messed things up this time?"

Kelli shook her head, trying to bring her mind into focus. "Rachel, what are you talking about?"

"Milo told me last night we're going to have to delay our honeymoon. He has to be in Dallas next week for meetings and some other Cowboys business."

"That's not the end of the world, Rachel; it doesn't change anything. Greg and I never had a honeymoon."

"Kelli, but you don't understand. I told Milo I'm pregnant, but I'm not." Rachel began to wring her hands. "I'm still trying to get pregnant, before he catches on. Now, we're going to be separated and now I don't know what I'm going to do."

Kelli knew she had not just heard what she thought she heard. She lost it. "Rachel Pettigrew, have you lost your natural mind!" she shouted.

Kelli's voice resounded throughout the women's dressing area. Of course, Mrs. Pettigrew heard it with her ear pressed against the restroom door, but so did the other bridesmaids and attendants waiting in the dressing area.

Rachel tried to hush Kelli. "Shh. Kelli, you're my best friend in the whole world and the only one I could tell. You have to help me."

A million things went through Kelli's head as she stood before Rachel with her arms tightly folded. Rachel had lied to trap Milo. Bianca was moving to Los Angeles with some co-worker she hardly knew. Now Rachel had the gall to say she needed Kelli's help. Kelli took several deep breaths, but her mind continued to race. She thought about the wedding party waiting in the dressing area. She thought of Milo, who had been played for a fool, but who had also played himself. She thought about the guests arriving—the family and friends, including her own husband, Rita and Able who would be arriving soon. It was when Kelli thought about Rev. Pettigrew and Mrs. Pettigrew, who would be most disappointed by their daughter's evil scheme, that Kelli was able to reach through her inner turmoil.

She grabbed Rachel tightly by the shoulders. "Rachel, you're a lying, conniving bitch! And I'm going to help you despite that. This is what you're going to do. While Milo's gone you're going to tell him you suffered a miscarriage. Then, do whatever the hell you want to do after that!"

Kelli turned and walked out the ladies room. She bumped into Mrs. Pettigrew on her way out. She changed into the hideous bridesmaid's dress and put on a phony smile for the ceremony.

Chapter 50
Kelli

Kelli Brown-Campbell graduated with a four-year degree in Accounting. She found a comfortable job with a small Ohio accounting firm. Kelli was pleased with her accomplishments, especially so in that she had never been a great student in high school. She diligently applied herself in college and reaped the benefits professionally and monetarily with a satisfying career.

Kelli and Greg were soon able to purchase their first home. Greg proved himself to be a skilled woodsman. He could build or fix anything made of wood. He added a sun porch onto their home and replaced all the wood cabinets and trimming throughout the house. He laid new wood flooring and built an intricate bookshelf in the family room.

Thankfully time began to heal the wounds in their marriage. As they collaborated on projects for the house, they began to talk. Strained at first, but eventually their conversations opened to include not just the plans for their home, but the dreams for their life together. One day they found themselves laughing together. Soon they kissed again and one day their passion returned. They found themselves renewed by their lovemaking and glowing in the tenderness that had survived the storm. It took some time, but eventually they talked about having children together and they prayed God would bless them.

Their first child, Chandler, a daughter, arrived two years after they purchased the home. The miracle of a child helped to make Kelli and Greg feel more like a real family. Three years later their son, Braxton, was born and their family was complete. Patty Campbell and Rita Brown were doting grandmothers. Able readily took on the role of Grandfather.

Kelli's life was centered on her family and she liked it just that way. While Fairfield was growing and expanding by leaps and bounds, it was still a great place to raise a family and Kelli was happy she and Greg had never decided to move. She liked the slow pace of the town and homey feeling. She wouldn't trade her life for any other.

Kelli maintained relationships with Rachel and Bianca over the years and accepted long ago, that Rachel and Bianca, although once childhood friends, were destined never to be friends again. Life moved on.

* * * *

Kelli's cell phone rang on her way home from work. Kelli tapped her Blue Tooth on.

"Hey, Rita," Kelli said to her mother who called nearly every day when she knew Kelli was on her way home from work.

"Hey, Baby. How was your day at work?"

"It was good, but busy. Hopefully that means job security. These companies are still laying off right and left and I'm just grateful to have a job in this economy."

"Yes, a job is a blessing."

"And how is the busiest woman in retirement?" Kelli asked of her mother.

"I just came in from water aerobics and I'm on my way to a darned ladies auxiliary meeting that I let Ophelia Pettigrew talk me into. I should've never told her I had Tuesday afternoons free."

Kelli laughed. "Mrs. Pettigrew never stopped with her auxiliary and women's day programs. Sounds like fun!"

"Well, it's not!"

Kelli could imagine Rita frowning on the other end of the telephone.

"Hey, Kelli. I wanted to know if you had some free time this evening."

Mentally Kelli flipped through her weekly calendar. It was Thursday and there would be no soccer practice for Braxton. Chandler would be busy with her Grandma Campbell at a scrap booking class they were taking together. "Sure. What's up?"

"I think I've found a condo and I'd like you to come take a look at it."

"That'll be great. What time do you want to go out?"

"I'm meeting the Realtor at 7."

"Great. I'll pick you up at 6:30."

"Okay, Honey. I'll see you then."

"Okay. Bye."

Rita had been looking at condos for the past several months. Kelli could hardly believe her mother would be moving out of her childhood home; the house her grandparents had owned. She felt nostalgic about the old house. Whenever Kelli dreamed of Grammy she dreamed of Grammy still healthy and moving around in that old house. She never dreamed about Grammy in the nursing home. Still, Kelli kept reminding herself: Life moves on.

Chapter 51

Rachel

Rachel Pettigrew-McFadden lived the lifestyle of the rich and famous. Her husband, Milo McFadden, NFL player with the Dallas Cowboys, was famous and they were truly rich. Rachel lived in a mansion; she had maids, servants and a personal assistant who waited on her hand and foot. Milo's parents and his younger brother, Maurice, moved to Dallas with them. The McFadden's lived a life of wealth and excess.

Yet, life was not without drama. Shortly after her marriage, Paris Cunningham, Rachel's friend and partner in crime from Ohio State, reared her ugly head. Paris threatened to expose Rachel as a gold-digging master manipulator. Paris demanded a half million dollars or she would take her story to the tabloids. Rachel hired an attorney to protect herself and Milo's image. Paris settled out of court for a fraction of the half million dollars she originally demanded. Still, it was not cheap getting rid of Paris.

After his retirement from professional sports, Milo was ready to start a family. Rachel remained determined to give her husband children, but motherhood eluded her. Her OB/GYN diagnosed her with endometriosis and sent her to a fertility specialist. She tracked her ovulation, bedded Milo when she was told and still, she never conceived. She remained haunted by the fact that Milo had conceived with a woman in his past, Bianca Goode. Rachel knew she was better than *her* and she remained convinced in her heart of hearts she would give Milo a house full of children one day.

Rachel would be "forever friends" with Kelli. They talked on the phone often. Kelli supported Rachel when she needed it and scolded her when she needed it, too. Rachel rarely returned to Ohio; instead she sent plane tickets for her parents to visit her in Dallas. Still, on the rare trips to Ohio, Rachel was certain to spend time with Kelli and her mother, Rita. They were a part of Rachel's family and would forever remain so.

* * * *

"So, what's that husband of yours up to these days?" Kelli asked of Rachel.

"He's more than ever determined to replace Tiger Woods as the number one golfer in the world. He spends nearly day and night on the golf course. He watches that mess on TV all day, too," Rachel laughed. "And what's Greg building these days?"

"Today he's working on a wooden bench for the back yard. Soon he'll be doing some work on Rita's old house before she puts it on the market," Kelli responded, and a tear formed in her eyes.

"Wow! I can hardly believe Rita doesn't live in the house next door to my parents anymore. Well, good for her. I've been trying to get my parents to move for years. With the money we have we've offered to buy them a new home, but they refuse. Now, don't get me wrong; Rev. Pettigrew accepts cash for a new Cadillac every year and Mrs. Pettigrew buys a new red sports car every year!"

"I know your Mom's a trip! She almost hit me one day speeding down the driveway when I was taking the kids over to Rita's house," Kelli laughed. "It might be time to think about taking away her license!"

"I'll assess the situation thoroughly when we're in town next month for the class reunion. They're giving Milo an award this year!"

"That's great. Greg and I are looking forward to seeing you guys."

"I'm looking forward to seeing those kids of yours. I can't believe Chandler is already in middle school and Braxton is a little soccer star."

"Yes, time stands still for no man," Kelli said.

"Or woman!" Rachel reminded her.

"True dat, true dat!" Kelli said to her old friend.

Rachel could hardly believe her godchildren were getting so big. She hadn't seen them in nearly four years. She would take a suitcase full of gifts for them when they went to Ohio. She still didn't have any children of her own, so she reveled in being a godmother. Kelli would get on her for spoiling Chandler and Braxton. Rachel would have to listen to Kelli's bickering, because there was no way she was going to Ohio empty-handed.

Chapter 52

Bianca

Bianca Goode had a rough start in Los Angeles. She did not break into the hair and make-up industry as readily as she hoped out west. Still, there were multiple ways for a pretty girl to turn a fast buck in the land of the beautiful people. Bianca found herself living off the kindness of men who appreciated her looks. She worked in the entertainment industry and found herself sliding down a pole. More money was literally thrown at her than she had ever seen in her life. As a new girl, she was able to book private parties and after-hour sessions with men who were willing to pay handsomely to take advantage of her midwest appeal.

During that time Bianca found Evan Smith. Evan was a not-so-handsome older man who specialized in entertainment of the sleazy kind. He was rich and white and had his hand in pornography and prostitution. Evan frequented the strip clubs in search of new blood for his business. Yet, when Bianca caught his eye, he desired her as a personal conquest. He wanted Bianca for his own. Evan offered Bianca a different kind of life. She would only have to dance for him, she would be his woman and he would give her anything she wanted. Bianca took Evan's offer. However, Bianca did not know Evan was an old-school pimp. He kept Bianca in line, by pumping her full of cocaine and when she got out of line he beat her senseless.

Bianca had to almost enter the witness protection program to free herself of Evan. She moved to Phoenix to escape his abuse. Eventually Bianca cleaned herself up and found a legitimate job. That's where she was when she encountered her old love, Milo McFadden.

Bianca was leaving work, the beauty parlor in an exclusive hotel, when Milo called her name.

"Bianca. Bianca Goode," she heard a familiar voice call her name.

She turned around to see Milo McFadden. The only man she had ever loved. Yet, their relationship had ended horribly. Milo had broken up with her on the telephone and stabbed her in the back by marrying Rachel Pettigrew.

She stopped, and when he approached, she could not resist. She reached up and hugged Milo, like nothing bad had ever happened between them. She looked Milo over. The years had been good to him. He looked as fit and handsome as ever. She noticed just a few grays poking out on his goatee and mustache, but they made him look like a grown man.

"What are you doing here, B?" he asked her, using his old nickname for her.

"I live here," she said brightly. "I could ask you the same thing."

"I'm here visiting an old friend. We use to play ball together and he's been diagnosed with cancer. He's dying," Milo said sadly. "I'm here to say goodbye."

"I'm sorry to hear that," Bianca replied genuinely.

"I'm on my way to the hospital, but can we talk later?" Milo asked, and took Bianca's hand in his.

Bianca was at a lost for words. She looked around and behind Milo.

He said, "I'm here alone, B."

She said, "I was just heading home and I..."

"I just want to talk," he said. "Let me buy you dinner this evening. Any place you name it and I'll have my driver pick you up."

Bianca couldn't believe it. Here was Milo McFadden standing in front of her. He had been the love of her life. He was in town alone and he wanted to talk.

They talked at dinner that night and so many more times after.

Chapter 53
Final Walk Through

Bianca showed up in Fairfield two days before the class reunion celebration where Milo McFadden would be honored. She called Kelli and told her she was at the airport and would be checking into a hotel. Of course, Kelli would not hear of it. She insisted Bianca stay at her house, but thought twice of it. Greg was stripping the wood floor in the guest room and they had moved all of the furniture out of the room into the basement. Then it dawned on Kelli. Rita's house was available. Rita had left the house partly furnished and it would be comfortable enough for Bianca while she was in town.

Kelli was elated to have Bianca home. It was nice to see her old friend and they had some serious catching up to do. They talked about their old classmates and which ones were supposed to be in attendance, according to Facebook updates.

"Did you see Tawana Tucker's profile?" Bianca asked.

"Yes, she was always so tall and so big, but now she looks like a supermodel!" Kelli squealed.

"Remember Rachel having it in for Tawana back in grade school?" Bianca reminded Kelli.

Kelli was surprised Bianca had mentioned Rachel's name.

"I remember the big purple bruise on Rachel's forehead from that tether ball incident!"

The two laughed all the way to Rita's house. When they arrived, Kelli helped Bianca with her bags and dropped them at the front door.

"Wow, it feels so funny being back here," Bianca said. "I have a lot of good memories of this old house. I wish I could say the same for the house I grew up in next door," Bianca said.

"I think about you every time I look at that house next door. Have you heard from Lilly?" Kelli asked.

"Yeah, she's fine. Her little girl is almost two now. I'm going to see her while I'm in town."

"Good for you," Kelli said. "What about your mom?"

"I haven't talked to my mom in years. I'm not even sure where they're living now. Probably back in a trailer park."

Bianca removed her jacket, exposing a very pregnant belly. Kelli couldn't believe she had not noticed it when she hugged Bianca at the airport. Sure, Bianca's face was full, but she just assumed Bianca had filled out. After all, they were forty years old.

"Bianca, you're pregnant! Why didn't you say something?"

"Surprise!" Bianca said. "I'm forty years old and having my first child!"

"I didn't even know you were seeing anyone."

Bianca sat on the sofa. "We have a lot of catching up to do. But, for now all I want to do is take a long hot shower and climb into bed. It's been a long trip."

Kelli let Bianca off the hook, because she did indeed look tired.

"Okay, but I'll be by first thing in the morning to pick you up for breakfast at my house with the family. Then we'll stop by the grocery and get you some food. Rita said there's nothing in the fridge. Plus, now that I see you're eating for two, we'll definitely have to stock up."

Bianca placed her arms around Kelli and hugged her

"Thanks, Kelli. You've always been the best friend ever."

"I'll see you in the morning," she said and Kelli was out the door.

* * * *

Kelli woke up early and started cooking breakfast. She sent a text to Bianca and told her she would pick her up in thirty minutes. It was a short ride to Rita's house and breakfast would still be warm. Bianca sent a reply text almost immediately and said she was starving and Rita was right, her refrigerator was empty. Kelli laughed aloud. She would be sure to stop at the grocery later.

Bianca sat back from the table and burped loudly, "That was great, Kelli."

Chandler and Braxton laughed at their Auntie Bianca. Their mother would never stand for them burping at the table without excusing themselves, but she never said a word to their Auntie.

After breakfast, Greg retreated to the backyard. Braxton went to the family room to play his Wii and Chandler headed for the computer. Kelli was grateful, because it would give her and Bianca a chance to talk.

"So, Bianca, who's the mystery father?"

Bianca responded slowly and deliberately, "Someone I've been taking it slow with. We're making plans."

"Good," Kelli said, sensing Bianca's apprehension. "Are you happy?"

Bianca thought about it and said, "Yes. I'm happy."

Kelli smiled and said, "That's all that matters. Becoming a mother is one of the most beautiful blessings there is in this world."

As if on cue, Chandler screamed at the top of her lungs from the family room, "Braxton, turn that TV down!"

Kelli and Bianca looked at one another and laughed. They were interrupted by a single ring tone on Kelli's cell phone. It indicated a text message had arrived. Kelli checked her cell and read a message from Rachel, *Plane just landed, headed to hotel.*

Coincidentally, Bianca received a text message immediately following Kelli's. She checked the message and then made an announcement.

"I'm ready to lie back down. Do you think I can borrow your car to go back to your mom's house? I'd like to run a few errands a little later as well."

"No problem." Kelli retrieved her car keys from her purse and handed them without reservation to Bianca. "You certainly wouldn't be able to get any rest around here this afternoon. These two children of mine get pretty rambunctious."

Bianca accepted the car keys and said, "I'll be back later this afternoon and maybe we can go and visit Lilly together."

"That sounds great," Kelli said.

Kelli busied herself with housework that was reserved for the weekends and rallied the children to do their chores. Half way through her list of things to do her cell phone rang.

Looking at the ID screen on her cell phone, she replied, "Hey Rachel, are you all settled into your hotel?"

Instead of a pleasant greeting, Kelli heard Rachel screaming and shouting into the telephone.

"Where the hell is she, Kelli? Where is that backstabbing prostitute, Bianca? I know you know where she's at!"

"Bianca? Why are you looking for Bianca?"

"Milo just told me he's leaving me for Bianca. That they're going to the class reunion together and they're going to start their life together like it was before! He talked as if this is the senior prom all over again!"

Kelli panicked. "Rachel, where are you?"

"I'm on the way to my parents' house! You don't think I was going to stay in that hotel with Milo for one more second, do you?"

Kelli thought, *Oh shit!*

"Rachel, I'll call you back!"

"What do you mean you'll call me back!" Rachel yelled. "Tell me where that lying, conniving Bianca is!"

Kelli hung up the cell. She found Greg's car keys on the top of his bedroom dresser. She took them and headed for the front door. On her way out she shouted back at the kids, "Tell your father I have his car and I'm going over to Grandma Rita's."

In unison, Chandler and Braxton said, "Okay."

Kelli knew they would not deliver the message.

Chapter 54

Breaking Glass

Kelli sped into Rita's driveway. She saw her car parked in the driveway, which meant Bianca was inside. A shiny new luxury car with out-of-state plates was in the Pettigrew driveway next door, so Kelli knew Rachel had arrived at her parents' house. Kelli hustled out of Greg's car and ran to the front door. She had to get Bianca safely out of Rita's house and away from Rachel.

Kelli was too late. She could hear Bianca and Rachel arguing inside, before she reached the door. Kelli burst through the front door and there they were, nose to nose and yelling at the top of their lungs.

"Milo is my husband! We're not high school boyfriend and girlfriend!" Rachel defended her marriage.

"Well, I had him first. You were jealous of our relationship back in high school!" Bianca threw the words in Rachel's face. "Now I've got him back and you can't do a damn thing about it!"

"Jealous!" Rachel said. "I'll show you jealous."

Rachel reached inside her coat pocket and pulled out a gun.

Kelli jumped between her two friends.

"Go ahead and shoot me if you think you have the balls!" Bianca shouts at Rachel, who is standing on the adjacent side of the cramped living room. Kelli struggles frantically to wrestle the gun away from Rachel. The oversized furniture in the tiny space leaves no room for their two thrashing bodies to maneuver without bumping into the sofa or loveseat. Still, Rachel is not detoured from trying to kill Bianca, despite their childhood friendship.

"No, Rachel, you don't want it to end this way!" Kelli begs. "Think about your future. You have too much to live for. Think about your parents. This will kill them! Your father's the pastor of a church. His only child can't spend the rest of her life in prison! Just think about it, please!"

Kelli sweats profusely as she struggles in a tug-of-war with Rachel, who is at least four inches taller and more than fifty pounds heavier than she. The two have already knocked two pictures off the wall and tumbled over a plant resting on a delicate iron stand.

"Rachel, you don't want to disappoint Mrs. Pettigrew and Rev. Pettigrew, do you?" Bianca teases, using a four-year-old's whining voice instead of that of a grown woman. "Oh, no, not their perfect little daughter with all of her fancy education, successful career and big bank account. Why, that would just devastate the perfect Pettigrew family."

"Shut up! You're just jealous because you're ignorant, unemployed and broke!" Rachel yells back at Bianca, cutting her to the core.

"Whoa! Such nasty words coming from the good pastor's daughter. Where did you learn that type of language—in Sunday school or bible study?" Bianca asks with an evil smile spread wide across her face.

Rachel twists her face harshly and replies, "The same place you learned to be a prostitute — from your stepfather!"

Bianca takes the argument over the top by saying, with a sad expression, "I'm surprised a barren bitch like you could come up with something so clever, yet so low down."

"No more!" Kelli shouts. Facing Bianca, she demands, "Bianca, shut your mouth, just shut up!" Then, turning her attention back to Rachel, she pleads, "Please, Rachel," as sweetly as honey dripping from her lips, yet never releasing her grip from the weapon. "Please put down the gun."

Rachel's eyes begin to water and a long stream of tears flows down her cheeks cascading black mascara onto her white silk blouse. As the anger releases from her body, it seems surrender of the gun is inevitable. Kelli is certain Rachel is beginning to return to her right mind. There is no way she can continue this farce of killing their friend.

Then Rachel speaks in a near whisper, "She thinks I don't have the guts. She thinks I won't do it." Just as quickly as the anger is released, it returns and Rachel announces with a steadfast determination. "But I will. I swear I'll kill her!" Rachel resumes her effort to regain control of the gun. With one swift movement, Rachel and Kelli tumble several feet and knock over a crystal lamp from a side table. It crashes onto the hardwood floor breaking into a million tiny pieces. As Rachel and Kelli fight for possession of the 9-millimeter handgun, Bianca stands in place with hands on hips, poking out her swollen belly, which holds her first child due in less than one month. You would think in such delicate condition, Bianca would set her butt down, shut her mouth and exercise some degree of common sense. But not her! Bianca has to show her behind, eight months pregnant and all.

All the while, Kelli wonders over and over again in her mind, *How did we get to this point? We all used to be best friends. We grew up on the same street and played together as children. Now here we are grown women and Rachel is waving a loaded gun around like it's a child's play toy. Bianca has the gall to egg Rachel on as if the gun is going to shoot out a stream of water instead of bullets that will cut through her flesh, destroying both Bianca and her unborn child. How have I let the two of them get me into the middle of their mess?"*

"Get out of the way, Kelli! You can't protect her now! This time she's gone too far! This time I'm going to kill this tramp and put her out of her misery!" Rachel demands.

Feeling like she's losing the battle for possession of the gun, Kelli turns to Bianca and yells, "Get out of here! I can't hold her back much longer. Get out of here now!"

A stubborn Bianca never removes her hands from her hips, never backs down. "I'm not going anywhere!" she announces defiantly. "Let her handle her business, Kelli. Let her do what she thinks she has to do!"

All at once Milo bursts through the door and rushes inside.

"Milo, help!" Kelli pleads.

Rachel takes her final stand; she gets the gun free and clear of Kelli's grasp and points it at

Bianca. Milo rushes to Bianca and stands directly in the line of fire between his wife and his mistress. Rachel sees his act of betrayal, his act of defiance and she decides, in the moment, he will suffer the ultimate sacrifice. Rachel squeezes the trigger and the bullet penetrates into Milo's flesh.

Bianca screams, "Milo!" His blood spews from his torso uncontrollably, and as the bright red puddle starts to form under his motionless body, Bianca registers shock. As she feels the life flow out of the only man she has ever loved, and the movement inside her swollen belly indicating life, Bianca's screams slowly reduce to a mournful, eerie, keening moan, lasting long after Milo's final heartbeat.

CPSIA information can be obtained at www.ICGtesting.com
Printed in the USA
238306LV00001B/1/P

9 781457 503559